MAY THE
FAITH BE
WITH YOU

MAY THE
FAITH BE
WITH YOU

ZONDERKIDZ

May the Faith Be with You

Copyright © 2015 by Zonderkidz

Requests for information should be addressed to:
Zonderkidz, 3900 *Sparks Drive SE, Grand Rapids, Michigan 49546*

ISBN 978-0-310-75345-2

Cover design: *Cindy Davis*
Interior imagery: *© PhotoDisc*
Interior design: *Kait Lamphere*

Printed in the United States of America

15 16 17 18 19 20 21 22 23 /DCI/ 15 14 13 12 11 10 9 8 7 6 5 4 3 2 1

HOW TO USE THESE DEVOTIONS

SCRIPTURE

Read the Scripture. You may also want to read the verses around it. These will help tell you the beginning and ending of the story.

MASTER MOMENT

These are great words that help give you the main idea of the devotion. You may want to read just these lines later to help remind you of what you learned. They will also remind you of God's love for you.

WAYS OF WISDOM

This section tells a bit about the story in the Scripture you already read.

USE THE FORCE

These words help you get started praying. Feel free to add to them or change them to fit you better. Remember, prayer is your time to talk to and listen to God. Sometimes you may even want to say, "God, I'm listening" and sit quietly waiting to hear from God.

DEVOTION 1

Aren't five sparrows sold for two pennies? But God does not forget even one of them. In fact, he even counts every hair on your head! So don't be afraid. You are worth more than many sparrows. **LUKE 12:6–7**

MASTER MOMENT

God cares for us more than we can imagine!

WAYS OF WISDOM

Jesus taught the people about God's love. He said God would love them forever. God cares so much about us! He even knows how many hairs are on our heads. He loves us that much! We should not have any worries.

USE THE FORCE

God, you love us a lot. Help me to remember that when I don't feel so loved. Thank you, God, for loving me so much!

DEVOTION 2

Jesus saw the crowds. So he went up on a mountainside and sat down. His disciples came to him. **MATTHEW 5:1**

master moment

God wants everyone to hear and understand his message.

ways of wisdom

Jesus was a great teacher. He taught men and women, boys and girls. People of all ages came to hear him. He used stories and ideas that people could understand easily. Jesus loved his heavenly Father and knew exactly what to say.

use the force

Jesus, I know I must choose to listen to you. Listening is a choice I make. I have to listen closely if I am going to understand. I will listen to your teaching. Help me to hear you.

DEVOTION 3

> The LORD had said to Abram, "Go from your country, your people and your father's family. Go to the land I will show you."
>
> **GENESIS 12:1**

MASTER MOMENT

There are many special people who love and trust God no matter what. We can learn from them.

WAYS OF WISDOM

God had a special friend named Abraham. Abraham was married to Sarah. They loved God and each other. They prayed to God often and God knew them well. God had an idea for how to say thank you to Abraham for his great love and trust.

USE THE FORCE

God, let my love and trust for you be as big as Abraham and Sarah's.

DEVOTION 4

I will make you into a great nation. And I will bless you. I will make your name great. You will be a blessing to others.

GENESIS 12:2

master moment

God was happy that Abraham believed his promises.

ways of wisdom

God blessed Abraham because of his faith. God was so proud of him! God promised Abraham a big family and lots of land. God rewarded Abraham because he believed in God and he believed God's promises.

use the force

God, your many promises to us are real and true! Family and friends can't always keep their promises, even when they really want to. I am thankful that you are different.

DEVOTION 5

So Abram went, just as the Lᴏʀᴅ had told him.   **GENESIS 12:4**

MASTER MOMENT

God chose Abram for a special job.

WAYS OF WISDOM

God talked to Abram. He told him to pack up and go to a new land. Abram did it! He took his wife and nephew with him. He did not ask questions, he just trusted God. God blessed Abram and changed his name to Abraham.

USE THE FORCE

Dear Lord, sometimes it is easy to understand what you ask of me. Sometimes it isn't so easy. Either way, I know I can trust your plan for me, God, because you love me!

DEVOTION 6

> Is anything too hard for me? I will return to you at the appointed time next year. Sarah will have a son.
>
> **GENESIS 18:14**

MASTER MOMENT

God can do anything. Even if it seems impossible, God can do it!

WAYS OF WISDOM

Abraham and Sarah were very old. But God said they would have a son! Sarah was so surprised that she laughed. She was nervous but happy. Could God really give them a son? Yes! God did it. It was a miracle!

USE THE FORCE

Thank you, God, for your miracles! Thank you for the joy of new life!

DEVOTION 7

> By that time Abraham was very old. The
> Lord had blessed Abraham in every way.
>
> **GENESIS 24:1**

master moment

God's plan to have Abraham's family grow big and strong did not stop. God's plans for us never end either.

ways of wisdom

Abraham always followed God's plan. He raised his son Isaac to love God too. Isaac was a part of God's plan too ... the plan to have Abraham be the father of God's people. So when Isaac was grown up, Abraham knew that whatever God told him to do with Isaac he needed to do.

use the force

God, I will not be old for a very long time. But I praise you that your plan for me is for my whole life. Thank you that you can see ahead for me and keep me on the right path.

DEVOTION 8

And he married Rebekah. She became his wife, and he loved her.

GENESIS 24:67

MASTER MOMENT

God leads people when they pray!

WAYS OF WISDOM

Abraham's sons grew up. It was time for Isaac to get married. Abraham sent a servant to look in his hometown for a nice girl who believed in God. The servant prayed for God to lead him. Sure enough, the servant met Rebekah. She was just the right one!

USE THE FORCE

I won't be getting married for a long time. When the time comes, I can trust you, God, to help me meet the right person for me. While I am growing up, you will lead me in all ways. Thank you, God, for leading me when I pray.

DEVOTION 9

A dinner was given at Bethany to honor Jesus. Martha served the food.

JOHN 12:2

master moment

God wants our love. Always be welcoming to him.

ways of wisdom

Jesus went to see his friends Martha, Mary, and Lazarus. Jesus knew he was always welcome in their home. They loved Jesus, and he loved them. Jesus was happy. It felt good for him to know that he was welcome to visit and stay.

use the force

You are always welcome in my heart, God! Help me to also be welcoming to others.

DEVOTION 10

But Isaac said, "Your brother came and tricked me. He took your blessing."

GENESIS 27:35

MASTER MOMENT

Choosing to be honest is very important.

WAYS OF WISDOM

Sometimes we want something so much that we will do anything to get it. Even tell a lie. But if we tell a lie, we will suffer for it. Jacob told a lie and was afraid to see his brother, Esau, for years. God wants us to tell the truth to each other and to him.

USE THE FORCE

God, sometimes it seems easier to make something up. I am afraid others will not forgive me. I think I will not get in trouble if I just tell a lie. But lies always bring more trouble. Thank you, God, for helping me to be honest.

DEVOTION 11

Stay with him until your brother's anger calms down. When he forgets what you did to him, I'll let you know. Then you can come back from there. Why should I lose both of you in one day?

GENESIS 27:44–45

MASTER MOMENT

Our choices can affect others and our future.

WAYS OF WISDOM

When we make bad choices, God still loves us. He will forgive us if we say we are sorry. But sometimes other people are not as quick to forgive us. They might be really mad! We should tell them if we are sorry.

USE THE FORCE

Thank you, God, for forgiving me when I ask. Thank you for helping me to say I am sorry to others.

DEVOTION 12

They will be like the dust of the earth that can't be counted.   **GENESIS 28:14**

MASTER MOMENT

God takes every promise he makes seriously.

WAYS OF WISDOM

God promised Jacob some wonderful things. God said he would give Jacob so many children and such a big family that Jacob would not be able to count them all! God said he would give Jacob the land he was on. God kept his promises.

USE THE FORCE

God, in many times and places you have made promises to your people. You promised to be with all of Jacob's children, so I know you will be with me. Thank you, God, for keeping your promises!

DEVOTION 13

I am with you. I will watch over you everywhere you go. And I will bring you back to this land. I will not leave you until I have done what I have promised you.

GENESIS 28:15

MASTER MOMENT

God talks to us in many ways!

WAYS OF WISDOM

Jacob had a dream. He saw a stairway with angels going up and down on it! Then God talked to him in the dream! God told Jacob that he would be with Jacob and watch over him wherever he went. God would bless Jacob and help him. What an honor!

USE THE FORCE

Thank you for talking to us, God. We can listen. We can talk to you.

DEVOTION 14

Jacob woke up from his sleep. Then he thought, "The LORD is surely in this place. And I didn't even know it."

GENESIS 28:16

MASTER MOMENT

God is there even when we don't know it.

WAYS OF WISDOM

Jacob had a dream. When he woke up, he was so happy. God had talked to him in his dream, and he had seen angels! Jacob thanked God. He said, "God is in this place, and I didn't know it!" We should remember that God is with us even when we don't see him.

USE THE FORCE

Sometimes I forget that you are with me, God. How could I forget? Your love surrounds me all day and all night long! How can I not notice? Thank you, God, for being with me!

DEVOTION 15

Jesus' disciples asked him, "... Was this man born blind because he sinned? Or did his parents sin?"

"It isn't because this man sinned," said Jesus. "... He was born blind so that God's power could be shown by what's going to happen." **JOHN 9:2–3**

MASTER MOMENT

Jesus is very compassionate. That means he cares a lot about people!

WAYS OF WISDOM

Again and again, Jesus showed how much he loved people. He wanted to teach people about his father's love. Every chance he had, Jesus helped, taught, supported, and blessed people in the name of his heavenly Father. He cared about people's pain.

USE THE FORCE

You bless me, Father! Help me to see that what others consider a problem may just be there so that you can show your glory.

DEVOTION 16

Some men came carrying a man who could not walk. He was lying on a mat. They tried to take him into the house to place him in front of Jesus.

LUKE 5:18

MASTER MOMENT

It is good to have faith-filled friends who help us.

WAYS OF WISDOM

Jesus was teaching inside a house. It was too crowded to fit anyone else. A man who lived nearby could not walk. His friends believed Jesus could heal him. They made a hole in the roof. They lowered the man from the roof into the house. They really wanted to get their friend to Jesus!

USE THE FORCE

I am thankful for my good friends, God! Mine have helped me in so many different ways. I pray that I many continue to be a good friend too.

DEVOTION 17

When Jesus saw that they had faith, he spoke to the man. He said, "Friend, your sins are forgiven." **LUKE 5:20**

master moment

Jesus will hear and answer the prayers of our friends too.

ways of wisdom

Four men loved their friend, and they believed God could heal him. They carried their friend to see Jesus. When they couldn't get in the door, they went in through the roof. Jesus liked their faith. He wanted to help the man walk. Jesus forgave his sins. The man stood up all by himself! It was a miracle!

use the force

Dear Lord, help my friends who need you. God, hear the prayers of my friends!

DEVOTION 18

After that, she couldn't hide him any longer. So she got a basket that was made out of the stems of tall grass. She coated the basket with tar. She placed the child in the basket. She put it in the tall grass that grew along the bank of the Nile River. **EXODUS 2:3**

MASTER MOMENT

Our lives are in God's hands.

WAYS OF WISDOM

Sometimes God is doing things that we can't see. When Moses was born, the slaves in Egypt had no idea that he was the one God had sent to help them. Moses' mother had to send him away. But God watched over him.

USE THE FORCE

God, you know exactly what we need to do. I pray that I may know your plans for me.

DEVOTION 19

> When the child grew older, she took him to Pharaoh's daughter. And he became her son. She named him Moses. She said, "I pulled him out of the water."
>
> **EXODUS 2:10**

MASTER MOMENT

Moses had no idea what big plans God had for him!

WAYS OF WISDOM

Moses' parents were slaves. But God worked it out so that Moses was raised by Pharaoh's daughter. He grew up in the palace! Moses saw how badly God's people were treated. He did not know that one day God would use him to rescue the people.

USE THE FORCE

Thank you, God, that someday you will use me and my gifts and talents to help others.

DEVOTION 20

The angel greeted her and said, "The Lord has blessed you in a special way. He is with you."

LUKE 1:28

MASTER MOMENT

God sent his Son Jesus to earth to be with us and to save us from our sins.

WAYS OF WISDOM

Mary loved and trusted God. One day, an angel named Gabriel visited her. She was scared! But the angel told her not to be afraid. He said, "God has given you special favor. You will give birth to God's Son."

USE THE FORCE

I praise you for your love, Lord. I will open my heart to you like Mary opened hers!

DEVOTION 21

Mary said, "My soul gives glory to the Lord. My spirit delights in God my savior. He has taken note of me even though I am not considered important."

LUKE 1:46

master moment

Remember that God can do anything!

ways of wisdom

Mary told the angel, "I'm not married yet. How can I have a baby?" Gabriel said, "With God, all things are possible." Mary believed it! She agreed to do what God was asking of her. She would become the mother of Jesus.

use the force

Whatever you ask me to do, help me to say yes. Help me to be brave like Mary.

DEVOTION 22

She gave birth to her first baby. It was a boy. She wrapped him in large strips of cloth. Then she placed him in a manger. That's because there was no guest room where they could stay.   **LUKE 2:7**

master moment

The Savior of the world was born in the least expected place!

ways of wisdom

Jesus is the Son of God. He is God in human flesh! He is greater than the greatest king. Yet he was born in the lowest of places. Imagine a manger surrounded by hay and smelly animals. That's where Jesus was born. Jesus is a Savior for everyone!

use the force

A place does not have to be fancy for wonderful things to happen there! God, happy birthday to your Son!

DEVOTION 23

An angel of the Lord appeared to [the shepherds] ... They were terrified. But the angel said to them, "Do not be afraid. I bring you good news of great joy for all the people." **LUKE 2:9-10**

master moment

When Jesus was born, the angels in heaven were just as happy as people on earth!

ways of wisdom

God's angels like to praise God! That is what God's angels did on the night Jesus was born. God had sent his Son to earth to teach about God's love. It was joyful news.

use the force

Sometimes I am sad. Help me, God, to remember the angels on Christmas night singing praises to you! I can praise you every day of the year. I will be filled with joy too!

DEVOTION 24

But the angel said to them, "Do not be afraid. I bring you good news. It will bring great joy for all the people."

LUKE 2:10

MASTER MOMENT

Jesus' birth was the most important news in the world!

WAYS OF WISDOM

Jesus was born to his parents just like you were. But his birth was the best news anyone could hear! Jesus would grow up and teach the whole world about God's love. Jesus came to save us from our sins.

USE THE FORCE

Thank you for the best gift ever, God! Help me to find ways to share this best news with other kids.

DEVOTION 25

Suddenly a large group of angels from heaven also appeared. They were praising God. **LUKE 2:13**

MASTER MOMENT

Listen, God has a message for us too! Jesus was born for all of us!

WAYS OF WISDOM

On the night Jesus was born, some shepherds were out in the fields. Suddenly, they heard and saw angels! The angels told the shepherds about the birth of Jesus. Think about how happy they must have been. They had been told for some time that the Savior would come. And here he was!

USE THE FORCE

Thank you, God, for the good news of Jesus' birth! I must pay attention, like the shepherds did. I will listen!

DEVOTION 26

Then the shepherds said to one another, "Let's go to Bethlehem. Let's see this thing that has happened, which the Lord has told us about."

LUKE 2:15

MASTER MOMENT

God wants us to be messengers for his good news.

WAYS OF WISDOM

After Jesus was born, the shepherds went to Bethlehem to see him. They were so excited! Then they helped spread the news! They wanted everyone to know that Jesus was the Savior. The Savior had come to earth!

USE THE FORCE

Dear Lord, I promise to tell my friends the good news of Jesus' birth. Everyone should be able to feel the hope of your promise to us.

DEVOTION 27

Naomi realized that Ruth had made up her mind to go with her. So she stopped trying to make her go back.

RUTH 1:18

MASTER MOMENT

Two are better than one. Two can share each other's burdens.

WAYS OF WISDOM

Naomi and Ruth loved each other. When their husbands both died, they decided to stay together no matter what. They became a good team. Life is more fun and easier when we are not alone. God gives us special friends who are always willing to help us. We should help them too.

USE THE FORCE

I thank you, Lord, for friends who share my burdens. Help me to be a good friend!

DEVOTION 28

Elisha replied to her, "How can I help you? Tell me. What do you have in your house?"

2 KINGS 4:2

MASTER MOMENT

God loves us, and he is bigger than our problems.

WAYS OF WISDOM

A woman was in trouble. She owed a man some money. But she didn't have any, so the man wanted to take her sons away. She needed help! She went to Elisha, the man of God. He knew that God was bigger than the woman's problem.

USE THE FORCE

Thank you, God, that I can always come to you for help! You will always show me to the help I need.

DEVOTION 29

The woman left him. Then she shut the door behind her and her sons. They brought the jars to her. And she kept pouring.   **2 KINGS 4:5**

master moment

Sometimes God does what seem like impossible miracles to help people!

ways of wisdom

A woman who owed money had only a tiny bit of oil. Elisha told her to put it into jars and sell it to make money. It wasn't enough oil, but she did not argue. The woman did what Elisha said. As soon as she poured the oil in the jars, there was lots of oil! It was a miracle!

use the force

God, you can do anything! Help me to remember that when I forget.

DEVOTION 30

Josiah did what was right in the eyes of the Lord. He lived the way King David had lived. He didn't turn away from it to the right or the left.

2 KINGS 22:2

MASTER MOMENT

It does not matter how old you are—God can use you.

WAYS OF WISDOM

Josiah was a little boy. He loved God very much. He became king when he was only eight years old. Can you imagine becoming a king? Even though he was young, King Josiah did many good things. He was a good example to the people.

USE THE FORCE

Thank you, God, that you use children to do big things! I pray that someday you will use me too.

DEVOTION 31

There was no king like Josiah either before him or after him. None of them turned to the LORD as he did. He followed the LORD with all his heart and all his soul. He followed him with all his strength. He did everything the Law of Moses required. **2 KINGS 23:25**

MASTER MOMENT

God loves it when the leader and all the people of the nation obey God's laws.

WAYS OF WISDOM

King Josiah was a good leader. His people followed his example. The people loved God and worshiped him. They promised to obey God's laws, just like King Josiah did. God was happy with King Josiah and the people for promising to obey him!

USE THE FORCE

Thank you, God, for nations and leaders who love you and follow your laws.

DEVOTION 32

Then Nebuchadnezzar was very angry with Shadrach, Meshach and Abednego. The look on his face changed. And he ordered that the furnace be heated seven times hotter than usual.

DANIEL 3:19

master moment

We are not to bow down to any other gods but the one true God.

ways of wisdom

Shadrach, Meshach, and Abednego knew their God was the one true God. They knew about God's rule that they only worship him. So they refused to bow down to another god. But that made the king of Babylon very mad.

use the force

Your rules, Lord, are for me to follow. No matter what! Sometimes it is hard to follow your rules today. Thank you for giving me faith to follow your ways.

DEVOTION 33

> The king said, "Look! I see four men walking around in the fire. They aren't tied up. And the fire hasn't even harmed them. The fourth man looks like a son of the gods."
>
> **DANIEL 3:24–25**

MASTER MOMENT

God protects the faithful.

WAYS OF WISDOM

Shadrach, Meshach, and Abednego were in trouble with the king. He made a big furnace very hot and threw them into the fire! But God takes care of his followers. The three men were not even burned! God sent his angel to protect them.

USE THE FORCE

Thank you, Lord, for protecting me. I know you take care of me, even in scary situations.

DEVOTION 34

Then Nebuchadnezzar said, "May the God of Shadrach, Meshach and Abednego be praised! He has sent his angel and saved his servants. They trusted in him. They refused to obey my command. They were willing to give up their lives. They would rather die than serve or worship any god except their own God."   **DANIEL 3:28**

MASTER MOMENT

God shows people who don't know him signs so that they can believe too.

WAYS OF WISDOM

The king threw Shadrach, Meshach, and Abednego into the furnace. He was amazed that they were not hurt! The king praised their God! He said everyone should know about how great God really is!

USE THE FORCE

God, you are great! Thank you for showing your power to me and to others.

DEVOTION 35

> Then they said, "Come on! Let's build a city for ourselves. Let's build a tower that reaches to the sky. We'll make a name for ourselves."
>
> **GENESIS 11:4**

MASTER MOMENT

We need God. We should not rely just on ourselves.

WAYS OF WISDOM

After the flood, the people started to forget how much they needed God. They got together to build a tower to reach heaven. But it was not what God wanted! The people were following their own plan. It didn't work.

USE THE FORCE

Dear Lord, I often tell other people, "I'll do it myself!" I know that sometimes you want me to do things for myself and other times I should rely on you. Thank you, God. I do need you!

DEVOTION 36

But the LORD came down to see the city
and the tower the people were building.

GENESIS 11:5

MASTER MOMENT

No one on earth is bigger, better, or smarter
than God.

WAYS OF WISDOM

After the flood, things changed on earth.
God helped the people start over again, but the
people became too sure of themselves. They
thought they knew better than God! No one
knows better than God! So God kept an eye on
his people.

USE THE FORCE

God, I often think I know better. I am sorry.
Please help me be mindful of myself when I
begin to think I know better.

DEVOTION 37

John is a witness to everything he saw. What he saw is God's word and what Jesus Christ has said.

REVELATION 1:2

MASTER MOMENT

Jesus told his disciple John all about the future. God wants us to look forward to the future.

WAYS OF WISDOM

One of Jesus' disciples was named John. When John was an old man, he had a vision. It was amazing! It was all about the future. In the vision, John even saw heaven! Jesus told John to write down what he saw in the vision and share it with God's people.

USE THE FORCE

Thank you, God, for a picture of my heavenly future!

DEVOTION 38

When Joseph came to his brothers, he was wearing his beautiful robe. They took it away from him.

GENESIS 37:23-24

MASTER MOMENT

God made families. Sometimes there is anger in families. But God will always love us.

WAYS OF WISDOM

Joseph's big brothers were angry at him. They didn't like his robe. They didn't like his dreams. They did not want him to be special. So they chose to do a very mean thing. They threw Joseph into a pit. The brothers forgot that each of them was special too.

USE THE FORCE

God, you made my family. Each person in my family is special. You want all families to live in peace. Thank you for helping me to show my family that they are special to me and to treat them with kindness.

DEVOTION 39

Jesus was born in Bethlehem in Judea. This happened while Herod was king of Judea. After Jesus' birth, Wise Men from the east came to Jerusalem.

MATTHEW 2:1

MASTER MOMENT

The heavens showed off the good news of the birth of God's Son!

WAYS OF WISDOM

When Jesus was born, there was a special star in the sky. It was really bright. It let people near and far away know that something special had happened. God wanted everyone to find out about the birth of his Son.

USE THE FORCE

I want to follow the light of your star, God. I will remember it when I need something to make me happy. Thank you for the special star!

DEVOTION 40

They asked, "Where is the child who has been born to be king of the Jews? We saw his star when it rose. Now we have come to worship him."

MATTHEW 2:2

MASTER MOMENT

The Savior is for everyone, everywhere.

WAYS OF WISDOM

Three wise men lived in a faraway country. They saw the special star in the sky. They knew the star meant that a Savior was born. So they decided to follow the star. They traveled a long way. They wanted to find the Savior.

USE THE FORCE

Thank you for showing us the right way, God. Keep showing the way to people all over the world.

DEVOTION 41

Shortly before dawn, Jesus went out to the disciples. He walked on the lake.

MATTHEW 14:25

MASTER MOMENT

Jesus did amazing miracles in his time. Amazing miracles happen today too!

WAYS OF WISDOM

While Jesus was praying, his helpers were in their boat. A big storm came. It was raining hard. It was so windy! The disciples were very scared. Then they saw something amazing. Jesus was walking to them. He was walking on the water!

USE THE FORCE

Thank you, God, for signs that show us you are with us today. Your miracles are amazing!

DEVOTION 42

"Lord, is it you?" Peter asked. "If it is, tell me to come to you on the water."

"Come," Jesus said.

So Peter got out of the boat. He walked on the water toward Jesus.

MATTHEW 14:28-29

master moment

Amazing things happen when we have faith and open our hearts.

ways of wisdom

The disciples thought Jesus was a ghost! Jesus' friend Peter needed proof. He said, "If you are Jesus, I want to walk on the water too." Jesus said, "Come." So Peter got out of the boat. He walked on the water to Jesus.

use the force

Jesus, you know that I can do more than I think. Faith in you is all I need. Thank you for helping me to believe in you, God.

DEVOTION 43

> But when Peter saw the wind, he was afraid. He began to sink. He cried out, "Lord! Save me!" ...
>
> Right away Jesus reached out his hand and caught him. "Your faith is so small!" he said. "Why did you doubt me?"
>
> **MATTHEW 14:30, 31**

MASTER MOMENT

Jesus' helping hand is always there to pull us up.

WAYS OF WISDOM

Even when Peter doubted him, Jesus still came to his rescue! Jesus was like that. He loved no matter what. He cared no matter what. Jesus showed how perfect God's love is for us. Jesus supports us through good and bad. He will always reach out to us if we ask.

USE THE FORCE

I am often afraid. I am afraid on the first day of school. I am afraid to join the team. Thank you, Jesus, for supporting me when I am afraid.

DEVOTION 44

When they climbed into the boat, the wind died down. Then those in the boat worshiped Jesus. They said, "You really are the Son of God!"

MATTHEW 14:32-33

MASTER MOMENT

Jesus wants us to trust him. Sometimes it might be hard. But he still wants us to try!

WAYS OF WISDOM

When Peter looked at the wind and the waves, he started to sink. "Why didn't you trust me?" Jesus asked Peter. Jesus helped Peter get back in the boat. Then the storm stopped. Jesus' disciples said, "Truly you are the Son of God!"

USE THE FORCE

Thank you, God, for sending your chosen one, Jesus. I know I can trust him with my life.

DEVOTION 45

Then Jesus told them a story.

LUKE 15:3

MASTER MOMENT

Jesus used special stories called parables to help people understand God's love.

WAYS OF WISDOM

People came to hear Jesus. They wanted to know who was most important to God. Jesus told the people a story. It was about a shepherd. Shepherds keep sheep safe. In the story, a sheep gets lost. The shepherd stops everything to find the sheep. This story shows that we are ALL important to God.

USE THE FORCE

God, you have lots of people to love! Still, I am important to you. If I get lost from you, you will come looking for me. Thank you for taking care of me like a shepherd.

DEVOTION 46

He spent everything he had. Then the whole country ran low on food. So the son didn't have what he needed.

LUKE 15:14

master moment

Even when we make a mistake, God loves us. He wants us to figure out when we are wrong.

ways of wisdom

A son did not make good choices. He did not pay attention to his money. He did not think about what his father might say to do. He did not think about what the Bible said he should do. He wanted to make his own decisions. He had a big problem.

use the force

Even as a child, I have to make choices. My parents can help me. I need to listen to them. Thank you, God, for helping me to accept responsibility for what I do.

DEVOTION 47

> Then he began to think clearly again. He said, "How many of my father's hired workers have more than enough food! But here I am dying from hunger!"
>
> **LUKE 15:17**

MASTER MOMENT

It is a good idea to stop and think. Pray and ask God for help. He always knows what is best.

WAYS OF WISDOM

The son had made a bad choice to leave home. Now he was in trouble. He needed to think about what was best. When we do not think about our choices, there can be problems! So the son sat down. He thought about what he should do next.

USE THE FORCE

God, help me to be mindful of my thoughts. Thank you for your wisdom.

DEVOTION 48

The son said to him, "Father, I have sinned against you … But the father said … "This son of mine was dead. And now he is alive again. He was lost. And now he is found."

So they began to celebrate.

LUKE 15:21-24

MASTER MOMENT

God welcomes us back when we are sorry.

WAYS OF WISDOM

The son went home. His father saw him coming! He was so happy. The son was sorry, and his father forgave him! Then the father threw a big party for his son. God is like that too. He is so happy when we say we are sorry for our sins. He welcomes us back every time.

USE THE FORCE

God, thank you for loving me no matter what.

DEVOTION 49

Those who accepted his message were baptized. About 3,000 people joined the believers that day.

ACTS 2:41

MASTER MOMENT

It is a great day when people say, "I believe in Jesus!" Think about how happy Jesus is to hear it.

WAYS OF WISDOM

Peter and the disciples stayed busy. The Holy Spirit lived inside them and helped them. They talked to many people about Jesus. On one day, three thousand people in Jerusalem said, "I believe in Jesus!" The disciples baptized each one of the new believers.

USE THE FORCE

Thank you, Jesus! I believe in you, Jesus! I pray the other people will believe in you too.

DEVOTION 50

The believers studied what the apostles taught. They shared their lives together. They ate and prayed together.

ACTS 2:42

MASTER MOMENT

Jesus' followers prayed together. It is good to be part of a faith family.

WAYS OF WISDOM

As more and more people heard about Jesus, the church grew. The disciples taught so many people about Jesus. They taught about being baptized. They taught about sin. The people wanted to stay together to learn more. They prayed with and listened to the disciples. Every day, more people believed!

USE THE FORCE

Thank you, Jesus, that I am part of a faith family.

DEVOTION 51

The believers studied what the apostles
taught.   **ACTS 2:42**

MASTER MOMENT

Large groups of people wanted to learn
about Jesus. The disciples worked hard to
teach them.

WAYS OF WISDOM

The disciples taught the people. They lived
with them and prayed with them. God had big
plans for people. God wanted them to know
how much he loved them. Jesus' disciples kept
teaching every day so more and more people
knew about Jesus.

USE THE FORCE

Your disciples teach me, Jesus, at home and
at church. Through prayer and Bible stories.
Thank you for disciples that teach me.

DEVOTION 52

I, your Lord and Teacher, have washed your feet. So you also should wash one another's feet. I have given you an example. You should do as I have done for you. **JOHN 13:14–15**

MASTER MOMENT

Jesus taught that when we love and respect others, we show God how much we love him.

WAYS OF WISDOM

Even though he was God, Jesus washed each of the disciples' feet. His friend Peter wanted Jesus to stop. But Jesus said he had to do it. Jesus wanted them to understand what it means to love and serve other people.

USE THE FORCE

Jesus, you washed your disciples' dusty feet. I can open the door for my mom when her arms are full of groceries. I can pull weeds with Dad. You gave me the example, Jesus. I will love and help others!

DEVOTION 53

Their hearts were glad and sincere. They praised God.

ACTS 2:46B–47A

MASTER MOMENT

Jesus' followers sang praise songs together. He loves to hear our voices raised in praise and joy!

WAYS OF WISDOM

Jesus' followers loved each other. They stayed together. They shared everything they had. They helped each other. They prayed and sang praise songs together. The disciples taught the followers about God and God's plans. Then the number of believers in Jesus grew and grew.

USE THE FORCE

Thank you, God, for my voice to sing praises to you!

DEVOTION 54

> Peter said, "I don't have any silver or gold. But I'll give you what I have. In the name of Jesus Christ of Nazareth, get up and walk."
>
> **ACTS 3:6**

MASTER MOMENT

Jesus' love is for every single person.

WAYS OF WISDOM

Peter and John and Jesus' helpers were busy teaching. They met a man who could not walk. Peter did not have money to give him. He only had Jesus' message of love. Peter gave the poor man the message. And the man was able to walk again!

USE THE FORCE

God, thank you for your message of love for me! There is nothing better. Not even silver or gold.

DEVOTION 55

All the people saw him walking and praising God.

ACTS 3:9

MASTER MOMENT

Jesus' message of love gives people strength. That's one reason why we need to tell them.

WAYS OF WISDOM

It was a miracle! The man could walk! All Peter did was tell him about Jesus and his love! Other people were watching. They saw the man's joy. They knew it was because he heard about how much Jesus loved him. They wanted to know more about Jesus too.

USE THE FORCE

Jesus, thank you for your love. Your love gives me true strength!

DEVOTION 56

When all the people were being baptized, Jesus was baptized too. And as he was praying, heaven was opened. The Holy Spirit came to rest on him in the form of a dove. A voice came from heaven. It said, "You are my Son, and I love you. I am very pleased with you."

LUKE 3:21–22

MASTER MOMENT

God the Father is pleased with his Son. He said so!

WAYS OF WISDOM

When Jesus was grown up, he asked John to baptize him. John was very surprised! But John baptized Jesus anyway. God spoke from heaven and said that Jesus was his son and he was very pleased with Jesus. Then the Holy Spirit came down as a dove!

USE THE FORCE

Thank you, God, for your chosen Son, Jesus.

DEVOTION 57

Blessed is the one who reads the words of this prophecy. Blessed are those who hear it and think everything it says is important. The time when these things will come true is near.

REVELATION 1:3

MASTER MOMENT

Sometimes God tells people about the future. We can learn more about God's plans this way.

WAYS OF WISDOM

God talked to John. He blessed John with a special message about his coming. John was told to write down every word he heard and about everything he saw. And he did! The book of Revelation tells us about what will happen when Jesus comes for us again.

USE THE FORCE

You have a plan for me and for all people. The plan is not just for today, but also for all time. Thank you, God, for your plan.

DEVOTION 58

Anna came up to Jesus' family at that very moment. She gave thanks to God. And she spoke about the child to all who were looking forward to the time when Jerusalem would be set free.

LUKE 2:38

MASTER MOMENT

God uses everyone to spread his good news.

WAYS OF WISDOM

Anna was 84 years old. She stayed at the temple all the time. She was praying and waiting for the Savior. She told many people he was coming. When Joseph and Mary brought baby Jesus to the temple, Anna knew he was God's Son!

USE THE FORCE

Like Anna, I want to tell others about Jesus. Help me to be brave and speak out to others.

DEVOTION 59

The LORD saw how bad the sins of everyone on earth had become ... But the LORD was very pleased with Noah.

GENESIS 6:5, 8

MASTER MOMENT

God loves people. Noah was one of God's very special people on earth.

WAYS OF WISDOM

So many people were not following God. God was sad that he had even created man! He had been so happy with them. He had said they were good! But no more. He decided that something had to be done to fix things on earth.

USE THE FORCE

I know that no people are perfect. If I need fixing, please know I am ready, God.

DEVOTION 60

So make yourself an ark out of cypress wood. Make rooms in it. Cover it with tar inside and out. **GENESIS 6:14**

MASTER MOMENT

Sometimes the jobs God gives us to do are hard work!

WAYS OF WISDOM

Loving God is not always easy. Sometimes God wants us to do big, hard jobs. God knew that Noah loved God. God knew that whatever he asked Noah to do, even if it was very hard, he would do it. Can you imagine having to build a boat big enough to hold two of every kind of animal? That would be a huge job!

USE THE FORCE

God, sometimes the work you give me to do is hard. Please ask me to help you! Please give me strength to do hard work for you.

DEVOTION 61

Two of every kind of bird will come to you. Two of every kind of animal will also come to you. And so will two of every kind of creature that moves along the ground. All of them will be kept alive with you.   **GENESIS 6:20**

master moment

God makes sure we have whatever we need to do his work.

ways of wisdom

God asked Noah to do a big job. God knew it would be hard. But he made sure Noah had all the right tools. He made sure Noah had all the right supplies. God wanted Noah to be successful on the ark just like he wants us to be successful in the jobs he gives us.

use the force

Thank you, God, for knowing the tools I need to do well. Thank you for giving me the best tool of all—my creative mind.

DEVOTION 62

Then the Lord said to Noah, "Go into the ark with your whole family. I know that you are a godly man among the people of today." **GENESIS 7:1**

MASTER MOMENT

When the people started to disobey God, he came up with a plan.

WAYS OF WISDOM

God saw all the people on earth being bad. He knew he had to do something to stop it. God had a plan. He would destroy humans and start over. He knew that Noah was a good man, so God asked Noah to help him save each kind of animal on the earth.

USE THE FORCE

God, when we disobey, you do not leave us. You do something. You make a plan. Thank you for staying with us.

DEVOTION 63

Noah was 600 years old. It was the 17th day of the second month of the year. On that day all of the springs at the bottom of the oceans burst open. God opened the windows of the skies.

GENESIS 7:11

MASTER MOMENT

God watches over us during both the calm times and the stormy times of life.

WAYS OF WISDOM

God helped Noah prepare. When the rains came, God made sure Noah was ready. God's plan was working. He was taking care of his people.

USE THE FORCE

God, sometimes the rain comes softly. Sometimes it comes with a crash and a bang. However it comes, rain is a gift from you for the earth. Thank you, God, for taking care of me: rain or shine!

DEVOTION 64

Pairs of all living creatures that breathe came to Noah and entered the ark ... Everything happened just as God had commanded Noah.

GENESIS 7:15–16

MASTER MOMENT

Noah trusted God to help him.

WAYS OF WISDOM

Noah followed God's plan. He built an ark. God said to put two of every kind of animal into the ark. But how were all the animals going to get there? Noah trusted God to provide for him. When the time came, God sent the animals to Noah.

USE THE FORCE

God, Noah worked with you to finish your plan. God, I trust your plan. Show me how I can help.

DEVOTION 65

The waters flooded the earth for 150 days.

GENESIS 7:24

MASTER MOMENT

God has perfect timing for all things. Waiting is not always easy for people.

WAYS OF WISDOM

Noah, his family, and the animals on the ark waited and waited and waited. They were floating on the ark for many, many days. But God knew what he was doing. He gave them all strength. He gave them what they needed to live. And finally the waters went down.

USE THE FORCE

Patience is a gift you give us, Lord. But waiting can be hard! Noah and his family were patient. Help me to be patient too.

DEVOTION 66

He waited seven more days. Then he sent out the dove from the ark again. In the evening the dove returned to him. There in its beak was a freshly picked olive leaf! So Noah knew that the water on the earth had gone down.

GENESIS 8:10–11

MASTER MOMENT

God lets us know when the right time has come.

WAYS OF WISDOM

When the rain was finally done falling, Noah needed to know. And God made sure Noah got the message. When it was right for Noah to leave the ark, God had a dove bring a branch back. The time to leave the ark had come!

USE THE FORCE

When the time is right, God, you will show me. If I wait for your sign, I will know.

DEVOTION 67

So God said to Noah, "The rainbow is the sign of my covenant. I have made my covenant between me and all life on earth." **GENESIS 9:17**

MASTER MOMENT

When God makes a promise, he always keeps the promise!

WAYS OF WISDOM

It rained for 40 days and 40 nights. It seemed like the rain would never stop. When the rain stopped, Noah prayed, "Thank you, God!" God said he would never again flood the whole world. He gave us rainbows to remind us of his promise.

USE THE FORCE

Thank you, God. Every time we see a rainbow, we remember your promise!

DEVOTION 68

Every year Jesus' parents went to Jerusalem for the Passover Feast. When he was 12 years old, they went up to the Feast as usual.   **LUKE 2:41–42**

master moment

God's Son grew up just like all kids do! He was a lot like you and me.

ways of wisdom

Jesus was God, but he was a human being too. He grew up like we do. He had a loving family. They did family things together like play, work, travel, and pray. So, Jesus knows what children go through.

use the force

Jesus, because you were a child like me, I know you understand my needs. Help me to let go of my worries and let you take care of me.

DEVOTION 69

They thought he was somewhere in their group. So they traveled on for a day. Then they began to look for him among their relatives and friends.

LUKE 2:44

master moment

Even as a young boy, Jesus wanted to be at the temple. It was the house of God.

ways of wisdom

Jesus was God's Son. So Jesus went to the temple. It was his heavenly Father's house! But he forgot to tell Mary and Joseph. Mary and Joseph could not find Jesus. They were very worried about their boy.

use the force

God, you made me a part of a family. Help me not to make my parents worry.

DEVOTION 70

They did not find him. So they went
back to Jerusalem to look for him.

LUKE 2:45

master moment

Parents won't give up looking when their
child is lost. God feels that way about us!

ways of wisdom

Mary and Joseph could not find Jesus.
They needed to know he was safe. They
looked everywhere. They refused to give up.
When we wander away, God wonders where
we have gone. God will not give up until we
are home safe.

use the force

God, I know you will not rest until I am
safe with you. Help me to not get too far away
from you.

DEVOTION 71

> After three days they found him in the temple courtyard. He was sitting with the teachers. He was listening to them and asking them questions.
>
> **LUKE 2:46**

MASTER MOMENT

We should love visiting God's house and learning all about God.

WAYS OF WISDOM

A house of God is where we learn about and worship God. It is a very special place. Jesus liked being at the temple. He felt comfortable there. He loved to talk about and worship his heavenly Father. He loved to talk about God's laws. He knew a lot about them.

USE THE FORCE

My faith family gathers together to worship you, God. We meet in a special place, set aside for you. I am glad to have a place where I can learn about you, God!

DEVOTION 72

In the beginning, God created the heavens and the earth.

GENESIS 1:1

master moment

God wanted something more. He wanted to share. God wanted to love, so he had a plan to make the earth.

ways of wisdom

God had his angels with him in heaven. And he was happy. But he wanted to share. He had a plan to create the world and everything on it and in it. This was so long ago, but he knew it was a good plan and he got started. So first he created the heavens and Earth.

use the force

Thank you, God, for everything in our great world that you have made.

DEVOTION 73

> The earth didn't have any shape. And it was empty.
>
> **GENESIS 1:2**

MASTER MOMENT

Only God can make something out of nothing! That is how he made the world.

WAYS OF WISDOM

God wanted to make the world. And he did it! It is amazing that he made it all out of nothing. Think about how hard it would be for you to make something out of nothing. It is impossible for you. But it is not impossible for God!

USE THE FORCE

Thank you, God, for creating the world! I can make a sand castle. With help I could build a tree house! But I can't make something out of nothing. Thank you for your amazing creation.

DEVOTION 74

God made the huge space between the waters ... God called the huge space "sky." There was evening, and there was morning. It was day two.

GENESIS 1:7–8

MASTER MOMENT

God created everything by himself. No one had to tell God how to do it.

WAYS OF WISDOM

God has a great imagination. He thought up every part of creation all by himself. He wanted to make things that made him happy. He had a plan to make people. His creation would make them happy too.

USE THE FORCE

God, you used your imagination to make our world. I am trying to imagine how you could create a whole world! Thank you, God, for your great imagination!

DEVOTION 75

God said, "Let the water under the sky be gathered into one place. Let dry ground appear." And that's exactly what happened. God called the dry ground "land." He called the water that was gathered together "seas." And God saw that it was good.   **GENESIS 1:9–10**

MASTER MOMENT

God just has to say the word and things are created!

WAYS OF WISDOM

God has great power. He knew what he wanted to create and so he did it! And the creations he made were just the way he thought they should be. Everything worked and fit into the world he was making.

USE THE FORCE

Thank you, God, for all you made for us. It is so good!

DEVOTION 76

> Then God said, "Let the land produce plants. Let them produce their own seeds. And let there be trees on the land that grow fruit with seeds in it. Let each kind of plant or tree have its own kind of seeds." And that's exactly what happened.
>
> **GENESIS 1:11**

MASTER MOMENT

When God made heaven and earth, he made things colorful.

WAYS OF WISDOM

It was God's idea to make things in the world have color. He chose to make the sun yellow, the grass green, and the sky blue. Imagine what the world would be like if it were only black and white!

USE THE FORCE

Thank you, God, for making the world colorful! Yellow bananas. Red roses. Cherry blossoms and sugar maple leaves: you made them all in color. Thank you for giving us a beautiful world.

DEVOTION 77

So God created the great sea creatures. He created every kind of living thing that fills the seas and moves about in them. He created every kind of bird that flies.

GENESIS 1:21

MASTER MOMENT

God created every kind of living creature.

WAYS OF WISDOM

Think about all the different kinds of living creatures. There is not just one kind of bird or one kind of fish! And he made all kinds of animals—reptiles, mammals, amphibians, birds, bugs, and fish. God thought of them all. Would you have been able to think of thousands of kinds of animals like God did?

USE THE FORCE

Thank you, God, for making long necks, wings, fins, legs, and tails!

DEVOTION 78

God made every kind of wild animal. He made every kind of livestock. He made every kind of creature that moves along the ground. And God saw that it was good. **GENESIS 1:25**

MASTER MOMENT

Animals have not always been around. God is the one who made them!

WAYS OF WISDOM

Think about your favorite animal. God was the first to think of that animal. He came up with the idea for dogs and cats, elephants and turtles. God knew his creation of animals was good. He knew we would love them. He wants us to promise to care for them.

USE THE FORCE

Thank you, God, for furry kittens and faithful dogs. Thank you for spotted cows and rumbling rhinos. Thank you for all of the animals!

DEVOTION 79

So God created human beings in his own likeness. He created them to be like himself. He created them as male and female. **GENESIS 1:27**

MASTER MOMENT

God's best creation was people!

WAYS OF WISDOM

People have not been around forever. God created man and woman. He designed them and gave them life. Think about all the people you know. Every one of them is different. And every one of them is special to God.

USE THE FORCE

Thank you, God, for making boys and girls. Thank you that people don't all look alike or act alike. Thank you, God, for making me just the way I am.

DEVOTION 80

The Lord God had planted a garden in the east in Eden. He put in the garden the man he had formed.

GENESIS 2:8

MASTER MOMENT

God gave man a beautiful garden to live in. He didn't have to do that but he loved man.

WAYS OF WISDOM

The Garden of Eden was great! It had everything people needed to live—food, water, beautiful plants, animal friends. And God was there too! He knew exactly what man needed.

USE THE FORCE

Thank you, God, for giving me everything I need to live. Help me to give thanks for them.

DEVOTION 81

The Lord God put the man in the Garden of Eden. He put him there to farm its land and take care of it.   **GENESIS 2:15**

MASTER MOMENT

God gave Adam a job to do. He has a job for each one of us.

WAYS OF WISDOM

God wanted Adam to take care of creation. He wanted Adam to name the animals. He wanted Adam to feed them. He wanted Adam to grow food for every creature that needed it. He taught Adam how to work.

USE THE FORCE

Thank you, God, for making us an important part of your creation. Help me to understand what my job is and to be happy doing it. Thank you for the work you give us to do each day.

DEVOTION 82

The Lord said to him, "Who makes human beings able to talk? Who makes them unable to hear or speak? Who makes them able to see? Who makes them blind? It is I, the Lord. Now go. I will help you speak. I will teach you what to say."

EXODUS 4:11–12

Master Moment

God gives us strength and courage. He can help us do anything.

Ways of Wisdom

When Moses grew up, God asked him to do a big job. God believed Moses could do it! Moses was nervous. He tried to get out of the big job. But God gave Moses courage. God knew Moses was the right person to help his people.

Use the Force

God, you teach us what to do. You help us every step of the way.

DEVOTION 83

So Moses got his wife and sons. He put them on a donkey. Together they started back to Egypt. And he took the walking stick in his hand. It was the stick God would use in a powerful way.

EXODUS 4:20

MASTER MOMENT

Sometimes it is scary to go to where God sends us. But God will help us be brave like Moses.

WAYS OF WISDOM

Like Abraham, God asked Moses to gather his family together. They traveled to Egypt. They were going to see Pharaoh. God gave Moses the confidence and help he needed. Moses was still nervous, but he knew God was there with him.

USE THE FORCE

God, I praise you for being my guide! I am sometimes scared to go to new places or to be around new people. That is ok. I have my family and I have you, God.

DEVOTION 84

During the night, Pharaoh sent for Moses and Aaron. He said to them, "Get out of here! You and the Israelites, leave my people! Go. Worship the LORD, just as you have asked." **EXODUS 12:31**

MASTER MOMENT

God's plans are for good!

WAYS OF WISDOM

Pharaoh was stubborn. He didn't care how much trouble he caused, until his own son was gone. Finally, Pharaoh yelled, "Get out!" Then Moses led God's people out of Egypt. God knew the plan was for good. God knew all along that his plan would work.

USE THE FORCE

God, you are powerful! I don't feel like I have much power, though. I praise you that you use your power only for good and that you can be strong for me.

DEVOTION 85

By day the LORD went ahead of them in a pillar of cloud. It guided them on their way. At night he led them with a pillar of fire. It gave them light. So they could travel by day or at night.

EXODUS 13:21

MASTER MOMENT

Even as God's people, we will face many challenges.

WAYS OF WISDOM

Pharaoh let God's people go, but then he changed his mind. He wanted Moses to bring the people back. Pharaoh chased God's people. They reached the Red Sea. They were trapped!

USE THE FORCE

God, I can't always do what I want to do. I feel stuck. I praise you for knowing where I need to be! Show me your way!

DEVOTION 86

Here are the laws you must explain to the people of Israel.   **EXODUS 21:1**

MASTER MOMENT

God knows we need some rules to follow. Rules help us remember what is good and bad. And they help us to live well with other people.

WAYS OF WISDOM

God led his people to a big mountain. He called Moses to go up to the top of the mountain. When Moses got there, God gave him ten special rules for his people. God wrote them down on tablets of stone.

USE THE FORCE

Thank you for your rules, God. The Ten Commandments are for me. I will follow my parents' rules too. Help me to have self-control and to live as you want me to.

DEVOTION 87

But the LORD said to Samuel, "Do not consider how handsome or tall he is. I have not chosen him. The LORD does not look at the things people look at. People look at the outside of a person. But the LORD looks at what is in the heart." **1 SAMUEL 16:7**

MASTER MOMENT

God knows that how we look is not the most important thing. God looks at our hearts.

WAYS OF WISDOM

God sent Samuel to see a man named Jesse. God told Samuel that one of Jesse's sons would be the next king for God's people. Jesse had eight sons. But it was not until Samuel saw the youngest son, David, that Samuel said, "That's the one!"

USE THE FORCE

Dear Lord, it is easy to worry too much about how I look or how others look. Help me to look at people's hearts and minds and not their clothes or hair styles. Help me to treat people with kindness no matter how they look.

DEVOTION 88

LORD, in the morning you hear my voice.
In the morning I pray to you. I wait for
you in hope.   **PSALM 5:3**

MASTER MOMENT

God wants his people to spend time alone
with him. He wants us to listen to what he has
to say.

WAYS OF WISDOM

To get to know God, we have to talk with
him. That's why praying is so important! We
can pray out loud or we can talk to him quietly
in our heads and hearts. God can hear us no
matter what! And when we listen very closely,
God answers us!

USE THE FORCE

Dear Lord, I am listening and ready to
hear you.

DEVOTION 89

She went away and did what Elijah had told her to do. So Elijah had food every day. There was also food for the woman and her family. The jar of flour wasn't used up. The jug always had oil in it. That's what the LORD had said would happen. He had spoken that message through Elijah. **1 KINGS 17:15–16**

MASTER MOMENT

God will always help the people who love him.

WAYS OF WISDOM

Would you share your last bite of food? A poor widow shared hers with God's servant, Elijah. It was so nice of her to help! Because she helped Elijah, God made sure that the food for her family never ran out!

USE THE FORCE

Lord, I always want more for myself. It is hard to share what I like. Help me to be more like the widow in this story, even if it seems hard.

DEVOTION 90

"I haven't made trouble for Israel," Elijah replied. "But you and your father's family have. You have turned away from the Lord's commands. You have followed the gods that are named after Baal."

1 KINGS 18:18

MASTER MOMENT

An idol is a false god. It cannot help anyone.

WAYS OF WISDOM

Some people put their faith in false gods. They believe that stone or wood statues have more power than the one true God! Stone and wood have no power at all. Only God can love and care for us the way he does. Only God can give us everything we need.

USE THE FORCE

God, you are the one true God! I can believe in a superhero, but it won't do any good. I pray that I remember the true God in my life every minute of the day.

DEVOTION 91

Jesus went up on a mountainside. He called for certain people to come to him, and they came. **MARK 3:13**

MASTER MOMENT

Jesus knew he needed strong and faithful helpers. Jesus wants us to be good followers too.

WAYS OF WISDOM

Jesus picked twelve men to be his special helpers. They were ordinary men. They were not famous men. Jesus didn't pick them because of how they looked or how smart or rich they were. Jesus knew they would be good followers.

USE THE FORCE

Jesus, you said, "Follow me." I want to follow you!

DEVOTION 92

Then the king gave a feast to honor Esther. All his nobles and officials were invited. He announced a holiday all through the territories he ruled over. He freely gave many gifts in keeping with his royal wealth. **ESTHER 2:18**

MASTER MOMENT

When we are beautiful on the inside, it shows on the outside.

WAYS OF WISDOM

The king of Persia was looking for a new queen. Esther was beautiful. She was kind. She cared about her family and the Jewish people. The king chose her to be queen! It would be a big job, but Esther would do it.

USE THE FORCE

Just like Esther, I have faith in the plans you have for me, Lord. I pray that I will have the patience to wait for your plans to happen.

DEVOTION 93

Godly Jews from every country in the world were staying in Jerusalem. A crowd came together when they heard the sound. They were bewildered because each of them heard their own language being spoken. The crowd was really amazed. **ACTS 2:5-7**

MASTER MOMENT

God's Holy Spirit helps us share the love of Jesus with others.

WAYS OF WISDOM

Peter and the disciples told everyone all about Jesus and his great love and sacrifice for the world. The people wanted to know Jesus too!

USE THE FORCE

God, help me to show your love to others! I pray that the Holy Spirit helps me believe what I don't understand and helps me to love others.

DEVOTION 94

Go to the great city of Nineveh. Preach against it. The sins of its people have come to my attention.　　**JONAH 1:2**

master moment

God is sad when people do bad things. He loves all people and wants them to be sorry for their sins.

ways of wisdom

God really wanted Jonah to go to Nineveh. The people there were sinning a lot. Jonah was one of God's prophets. God wanted Jonah to teach the people about God's love and mercy. But Jonah did not want to go. He didn't like the people of Nineveh.

use the force

God, send people to teach me your Word, just as you sent Jonah. Help me to do what you want when you ask me to.

DEVOTION 95

> But Jonah ran away from the LORD. He headed for Tarshish. So he went down to the port of Joppa. There he found a ship that was going to Tarshish. He paid the fare and went on board. Then he sailed for Tarshish. He was running away from the LORD. **JONAH 1:3**

MASTER MOMENT

We can try to run away from God, but he always knows exactly where we are!

WAYS OF WISDOM

Sometimes we just do not want to listen to God. Sometimes it feels easier to walk away from God. Being good and doing the right thing all the time is not always easy or fun. That is how Jonah felt. He did not want to go to Nineveh, so he ran away. But when God has a plan for us, we can't hide from him!

USE THE FORCE

God, help me find my way home if I run away. I know as long as I have you I will not be alone.

DEVOTION 96

But the LORD sent a strong wind over the Mediterranean Sea. A wild storm came up. It was so wild that the ship was in danger of breaking apart.

JONAH 1:4

MASTER MOMENT

God sometimes sends storms into our lives. He wants us to stop, think, and turn around!

WAYS OF WISDOM

Storms can be scary. There is heavy rain and wild wind! The sailors on Jonah's boat were scared. God did not want to hurt them. He wanted Jonah to get his message loud and clear! God wanted Jonah to do his will as he had told him to.

USE THE FORCE

I am listening, God. Help me to really hear. Help me to be a better listener.

DEVOTION 97

> They found out he was running away from the LORD. That's because he had told them. Then they became terrified. So they asked him, "How could you do a thing like that?" **JONAH 1:10**

MASTER MOMENT

The sooner we realize what God is trying to tell us, the better!

WAYS OF WISDOM

We need to keep our hearts open to God. Jonah knew that, but he forgot for a little while. When he saw the storm, he knew God was serious. Jonah knew God wanted him to do a job. He could not ignore God when so many people were in danger. Jonah knew what he had to do!

USE THE FORCE

God, my heart and ears are open to your will.

DEVOTION 98

Now the LORD sent a huge fish to swallow Jonah. And Jonah was in the belly of the fish for three days and three nights.

JONAH 1:17

MASTER MOMENT

God sent a big fish to rescue Jonah! God had a plan for Jonah. He has a plan for us too.

WAYS OF WISDOM

God did not let Jonah drown in the sea! A huge fish came along and swallowed him. It was amazing. Jonah was inside the fish for three days and three nights. It must have been scary, but Jonah knew that God was in charge. Jonah knew that God knew what he was doing!

USE THE FORCE

You rescue me too, God. You rescued Daniel and Jonah in different ways, but both were part of your saving plan. I praise you!

DEVOTION 99

The LORD gave the fish a command. And it spit Jonah up onto dry land.

JONAH 2:10

MASTER MOMENT

When Jonah was ready to obey God, God told the big fish to spit out Jonah.

WAYS OF WISDOM

Jonah spent his time inside the fish praying. He told God he was sorry. He promised to follow God's plan. God knew that Jonah was really sorry. He knew his prophet was ready to do God's work in Nineveh. Jonah was God's best man for the job. So God told the fish to spit Jonah out.

USE THE FORCE

God, you gave the lions in the den a command to keep their mouths closed. You gave the big fish a command to open its mouth. They did as you commanded. You are the God of all creation! I praise you!

DEVOTION 100

Jonah obeyed the LORD. He went to Nineveh. It was a very large city. In fact, it took about three days to go through it.

JONAH 3:3

MASTER MOMENT

Jonah was glad to be alive! He'd learned his lesson. He had a new attitude!

WAYS OF WISDOM

Jonah was thankful God had given him a chance to change his mind about going to Nineveh. He promised to share God's love. Jonah understood that God was serious about helping the people in Nineveh.

USE THE FORCE

I want to fill my attitude with gratitude! I am glad to be alive! God, I want to help you like Jonah helped you!

DEVOTION 101

God saw what they did. He saw that they stopped doing what was evil. So he took pity on them. He didn't destroy them as he had said he would.

JONAH 3:10

MASTER MOMENT

God forgave the people of Nineveh. He will forgive anyone who is really sorry! He forgives us!

WAYS OF WISDOM

Jonah told the people in Nineveh that God would destroy their city! They needed to start acting better. The people believed God's word and warning. They said they were sorry and would change their ways. The king heard God's word, and he changed too! God's plan was successful.

USE THE FORCE

God, your forgiveness and mercy are so great! You could have only punished Ninevah, but you gave them a chance to change. Thank you for also being so patient with me.

DEVOTION 102

> [Jesus] said, "What I'm about to tell you is true. That poor widow has put more into the offering box than all the others ... She put in everything she had. That was all she had to live on."
>
> **MARK 12:43–44**

MASTER MOMENT

Jesus knows when we give all we have. He knows what is in our hearts.

WAYS OF WISDOM

Jesus told his helpers to watch a poor widow. She put all the money she had in the box for the temple! Jesus said she put in more than all the other people did. It was a true sacrifice.

USE THE FORCE

God, please help me to understand what sacrifice means. Help me to know what I should give up and what I should keep.

DEVOTION 103

Israel loved Joseph more than any of his other sons. That's because Joseph had been born to him when he was old. Israel made him a beautiful robe.

GENESIS 37:3

MASTER MOMENT

God does not have favorites.

WAYS OF WISDOM

Joseph was Jacob's favorite son. Jacob made a colorful robe for Joseph. He wanted Joseph to feel special. Did you know that each and every one of us is very, very special to God? God loves all of his children very much. God does not have a favorite like Jacob did.

USE THE FORCE

God, you love each and every one of us so very much! You don't have a favorite. Thank you that I don't have to wonder that about you, God.

DEVOTION 104

[Joseph] said to them, "Listen to the dream I had. We were tying up bundles of grain out in the field. Suddenly my bundle rose and stood up straight. Your bundles gathered around my bundle and bowed down to it."   **GENESIS 37:5-7**

MASTER MOMENT

God speaks to his people in different ways. Sometimes he speaks through people's dreams.

WAYS OF WISDOM

Joseph told his brothers about one of his dreams. The dream made it sound like Joseph thought he was better than his brothers. The brothers were not happy about the dream. Why would this little boy have such a dream?

USE THE FORCE

Dear Lord, if there is something I need to know from my dreams, please help me to understand. Help me to know if my dream is from you.

DEVOTION 105

His brothers said to him, "Do you plan to be king over us? Will you really rule over us?" So they hated him even more because of his dream. They didn't like what he had said. **GENESIS 37:8**

MASTER MOMENT

We should think about other people's feelings.

WAYS OF WISDOM

Sometimes brothers get angry at brothers. Sometimes they do not listen very well to each other. And sometimes they do not really care. Joseph told his brothers about his dream and they thought he was bragging. The brothers were not happy.

USE THE FORCE

God, open my heart to how others feel.

DEVOTION 106

When Joseph came to his brothers, he was wearing his beautiful robe. They took it away from him. And they threw him into the well. The well was empty. There wasn't any water in it.

GENESIS 37:23–24

MASTER MOMENT

Sometimes people will dislike us unfairly.

WAYS OF WISDOM

Without even understanding the whole story, Joseph's brothers decided to do something wrong. They did something that could hurt their little brother Joseph! No one even took the time to talk to Joseph about the problem!

USE THE FORCE

God, sometimes others dislike me for no reason. I know you want me to forgive those who dislike me unfairly. But sometimes it feels so hard! Help me to forgive others.

DEVOTION 107

What Jesus did here in Cana in Galilee was the first of his signs. Jesus showed his glory by doing this sign. And his disciples believed in him.

JOHN 2:11

MASTER MOMENT

Jesus does miracles to teach people about God's love.

WAYS OF WISDOM

At a wedding, Jesus told the servants to fill up some jugs with water. Then he told them to dip some out into a cup and take it to their master. They did what he said. When the master took a sip, it wasn't water. It was wine. It was a miracle!

USE THE FORCE

God, you do miracles every day. Thank you for showing yourself to us in amazing ways.

DEVOTION 108

The commander replied, "Lord, I am not good enough to have you come into my house. But just say the word, and my servant will be healed."

MATTHEW 8:8

master moment

Some people are filled with faith in God. God wants us to be filled with faith too.

ways of wisdom

An army captain asked Jesus to help his sick servant. Jesus wanted to go to the captain's house to heal the man. But the captain said, "Just say the word and he will be fine." Jesus was amazed that the captain had such great faith in him.

use the force

God, help me to have as much faith as the captain!

DEVOTION 109

Jesus got into a boat. His disciples followed him. Suddenly a terrible storm came up on the lake. The waves crashed over the boat. But Jesus was sleeping.

MATTHEW 8:23-24

MASTER MOMENT

We have to trust in the Lord even when times get rough.

WAYS OF WISDOM

It was time for Jesus and his helpers to go across the sea. They got into a boat. Jesus took a nap. Suddenly, there was a really big storm! Jesus' helpers were scared. They thought the boat was going to sink.

USE THE FORCE

Jesus, please help me to be as calm as you were in that storm. I do not need to fear with you nearby.

DEVOTION 110

The disciples went and woke him up. They said, "Lord! Save us! We're going to drown!" He replied, "Your faith is so small! Why are you so afraid?"

MATTHEW 8:25–26

MASTER MOMENT

Even the most faithful forget sometimes.

WAYS OF WISDOM

Jesus' helpers were upset. The storm was scary. They woke up Jesus and shouted, "The boat is sinking! Don't you care?" Jesus said, "Why are you so afraid? Don't you have any faith?" Then Jesus told the storm to stop.

USE THE FORCE

I know you understand my fears, God. I know that you are with me. Help me never to forget.

DEVOTION III

Then Jesus got up and ordered the winds and the waves to stop. It became completely calm. The disciples were amazed. They asked, "What kind of man is this? Even the wind and the waves obey him!"

MATTHEW 8:26B–27

MASTER MOMENT

Relax and know that we are safe with Jesus.

WAYS OF WISDOM

When Jesus told the storm to stop, the water became calm. The storm was gone! The disciples couldn't believe it. It was a miracle! Everyone was safe. Jesus was right. With him in the boat, they had nothing to fear.

USE THE FORCE

You truly are the Savior, Jesus! Praise God that you always keep us safe.

DEVOTION 112

"I'm going out to fish," Simon Peter told them. They said, "We'll go with you." So they went out and got into the boat. That night they didn't catch anything.

JOHN 21:3

master moment

Don't forget about God when you go about your ordinary life. He can help.

ways of wisdom

The disciples had to make a living. One day, the men were fishing. They were not catching any fish. They were good fishermen, but not that day! What could they do?

use the force

Some days the things I do turn out right. Some days, everything is a big mess. No matter how it is going, Lord, I will place my trust in you!

DEVOTION 113

Early in the morning, Jesus stood on the shore. But the disciples did not realize that it was Jesus.

He called out to them, "Friends, don't you have any fish?"

"No," they answered.

JOHN 21:4–5

MASTER MOMENT

If we love Jesus, we should tell people all about him!

WAYS OF WISDOM

The man on the shore shouted, "Put your net in the water on the other side of the boat." Peter and his men did it. Then the net was full of fish! The man on the shore was Jesus. Jesus told Peter, "If you love me, take care of the people. Teach them about me."

USE THE FORCE

Jesus, thank you for giving me a really important way to take care of others—to tell them about you!

DEVOTION 114

The LORD God gave the man a command. He said, "You may eat fruit from any tree in the garden. But you must not eat the fruit from the tree of the knowledge of good and evil.

GENESIS 2:16–17

MASTER MOMENT

God told Adam and Eve not to eat from one tree in the garden.

WAYS OF WISDOM

God wants what is best for us. He wants to protect us from things that could be bad for us. Whenever God tells us not to do something, it is for a good reason.

USE THE FORCE

Thank you, God, for protecting me from every danger. Help me to remember that you know what is best for me.

DEVOTION 115

The serpent was more clever than any of the wild animals the Lᴏʀᴅ God had made. The serpent said to the woman, "Did God really say, 'You must not eat fruit from any tree in the garden'?"

GENESIS 3:1

MASTER MOMENT

God has an enemy. The enemy's name is Satan. He is also called the devil. You cannot trust him.

WAYS OF WISDOM

Satan is a bad guy. He does not love God. He disguised himself as a snake. He had a plan to hurt God. He planned on using Adam and Eve to help him. Adam and Eve did not know about Satan.

USE THE FORCE

Thank you, God, for protecting me from Satan. Thank you, God, for showing me who I should trust.

DEVOTION 116

The woman said to the serpent, "... God did say, 'You must not eat the fruit from the tree in the middle of the garden. Do not even touch it. If you do, you will die.'"

"You will certainly not die," the serpent said to the woman.

GENESIS 3:2–4

master moment

The devil tricked Eve into disobeying God and doing something wrong.

ways of wisdom

Has anyone ever tried to get you to do something bad? God and your parents are always watching out for you. They love you and want you to be safe. They want you to always do what is right.

use the force

God, help me not to be tricked into disobeying you. It is sometimes hard to say "no" to other kids who don't know you. You are always watching out for me. Thank you!

DEVOTION 117

The woman saw that the tree's fruit was good to eat and pleasing to look at. She also saw that it would make a person wise.   **GENESIS 3:6**

master moment

Things that look good are not always good for you.

ways of wisdom

God gave Adam and Eve the beautiful garden. They loved to look at everything God gave them. They were curious just like we are. But we remember something very important. God knows what is good for us. We need to believe God if he says something is not good.

use the force

Thank you, God, that you know what is good for me. I believe in you, God.

123

DEVOTION 118

She took some of the fruit and ate it. She also gave some to her husband, who was with her. And he ate it. Then both of them knew things they had never known before.

GENESIS 3:6A–7

MASTER MOMENT

Adam and Eve could not hide their bad choice from God. We cannot hide either.

WAYS OF WISDOM

Adam and Eve were told not to eat the fruit. When they did, something happened! God was very unhappy. The serpent had lied to them. It was not good knowledge they got after eating from the Tree of Knowledge.

USE THE FORCE

Thank you, God, for telling me the truth. I will be open and honest with you.

DEVOTION 119

The man said, "It's the fault of the woman you put here with me. She gave me some fruit from the tree. And I ate it."

GENESIS 3:12

MASTER MOMENT

When we do something bad, we are responsible. It does not help to blame someone else.

WAYS OF WISDOM

God gave Adam and Eve everything they needed. But they wanted more. We are responsible for what we do. God made sure that Adam, Eve, and Satan understood that.

USE THE FORCE

Thank you, God, for helping me learn right from wrong. It feels easy to blame others when I am ashamed of something I have done. I know I am responsible for what I do.

DEVOTION 120

So the Lord God drove the man out of the Garden of Eden. He sent the man to farm the ground he had been made from.

GENESIS 3:23

master moment

God knows when we do something wrong and disobey him.

ways of wisdom

God sees and knows everything. We cannot hide anything from God! He even knows what we are thinking and feeling. Whatever we do, God knows it. Adam and Eve tried to hide from God, but he already knew what they had done. And he punished them.

use the force

God, you know everything and still love me! I can't hide from you and I don't need to. Thank you.

DEVOTION 121

The people of Israel saw the flakes. They asked each other, "What's that?" They didn't know what it was. Moses said to them, "It's the bread the LORD has given you to eat." **EXODUS 16:15**

MASTER MOMENT

God does not promise that every day will be easy, but he loves us and will always help us.

WAYS OF WISDOM

God led his people into the desert. They were free, but they ran out of food. They were hungry! Then God showed his people how much he loved them. He sent bread down from heaven. It was called manna. No one had ever seen it before.

USE THE FORCE

God, thank you for making sure my family has what we need to live.

DEVOTION 122

As Jesus went along, he saw a man who was blind. He had been blind since he was born.   **JOHN 9:1**

MASTER MOMENT

Jesus cares about people. He wants us to care about other people too.

WAYS OF WISDOM

Jesus and his helpers saw a blind man. The man was asking people for food or money. Jesus went to the blind man. He made some mud and put it on the man's eyes. "Go to the pool. Wash the mud off," Jesus told the man.

USE THE FORCE

Jesus, you care about us all. I pray that I may always be caring just like you.

DEVOTION 123

Jesus said, "You have now seen him. In fact, he is the one speaking with you."

Then the man said, "Lord, I believe." And he worshiped him.

JOHN 9:37–38

MASTER MOMENT

When Jesus did miracles, people wanted to know more about him.

WAYS OF WISDOM

The blind man felt silly with mud on his eyes. But he did what Jesus said. He went to the pool and washed his face. As soon as the mud was gone, he could see! Everyone was amazed. They all wanted to find out more about Jesus.

USE THE FORCE

Jesus, you always have a way to make us well. You help me see you clearly like the blind man did! Thank you so much for your healing.

DEVOTION 124

Then Jesus said, "I am the bread of life. Whoever comes to me will never go hungry. And whoever believes in me will never be thirsty."   **JOHN 6:35**

MASTER MOMENT

We need bread to live. Jesus is the Bread of Life!

WAYS OF WISDOM

Jesus shared the Passover meal with his best friends. But this Passover meal was extra special. It was Jesus' last supper with his friends. Jesus held up the bread and told his friends that he was the bread that came down from heaven.

USE THE FORCE

Jesus, you are the Bread of Life! Praise God for the life you give.

DEVOTION 125

> Then he took a cup. He gave thanks and handed it to them. He said, "All of you drink from it. This is my blood of the covenant. It is poured out to forgive the sins of many people."
>
> **MATTHEW 26:27–28**

master moment

Jesus' life was poured out for us.

Ways of Wisdom

Jesus held up a cup of wine. He wanted his best friends to remember something important. He was giving up his life so people could have their sins forgiven and live with him in heaven. He told his friends to let the wine remind them of that.

Use the Force

Jesus, yours is the cup that saves! I want to drink from it forever.

DEVOTION 126

> Hold out your walking stick. Reach out your hand over the Red Sea to part the water. Then the people can go through the sea on dry ground.
>
> **EXODUS 14:16**

MASTER MOMENT

No matter how big the challenge, God has an answer for it!

WAYS OF WISDOM

Moses helped God's people in Egypt, but now they were trapped at the Red Sea. They had nowhere to go. But that didn't stop God! He did something no one had ever seen before. He parted the Red Sea! He helped Moses get the people across the sea to safety.

USE THE FORCE

You are amazing, God. I will never be trapped. You will help me find my way!

DEVOTION 127

You will receive power when the Holy Spirit comes on you. Then you will tell people about me from one end of the earth to the other.

ACTS 1:7–8

MASTER MOMENT

After Jesus went to heaven, the disciples remembered things he had said to them before.

WAYS OF WISDOM

Jesus was gone, but the disciples did not forget him. They remembered things Jesus had taught them. Jesus told them to teach people all over the world about God's love. So the disciples talked and prayed. They made plans. They followed Jesus' example. They decided to teach others.

USE THE FORCE

God, I want to be a good example of your love. Please let me have chances to tell other people about your Son.

DEVOTION 128

Saul got up from the ground. He opened his eyes, but he couldn't see.

ACTS 9:8

MASTER MOMENT

Sometimes Jesus has to be tough on people. He really wants them to hear and understand his Word.

WAYS OF WISDOM

Saul was a mean man. A bright light flashed and he fell down. He heard Jesus' voice. Jesus wanted him to stop being mean to God's people. He wanted Saul to help people believe in Jesus. When Saul got up, he could not see. He was blind.

USE THE FORCE

Please do not let me be blind to your message of love, God.

DEVOTION 129

For three days he was blind. He didn't eat or drink anything.   **ACTS 9:9**

MASTER MOMENT

While Saul was not able to see, he prayed. We do not need anything so big to start us thinking about God's love!

WAYS OF WISDOM

Saul was blind for three days. During those three days Saul prayed, fasted, and thought hard about God. During that thinking and praying time, Saul realized that God had a special job for him. God's plan was for him to teach the world about Jesus through traveling, preaching, and writing.

USE THE FORCE

God, help me to know my talents. They are to be used for your glory.

DEVOTION 130

Then Ananias went to the house and entered it. He placed his hands on Saul. "Brother Saul," he said, "you saw the Lord Jesus. He appeared to you on the road as you were coming here. He has sent me so that you will be able to see again. You will be filled with the Holy Spirit." **ACTS 9:17**

MASTER MOMENT

Saul became an important helper for Jesus on earth. We can be important helpers too.

WAYS OF WISDOM

Saul needed help getting to a city. A man named Ananias was in the city. Jesus told Ananias to go to Saul. Ananias prayed for Saul to see. Then Ananias baptized Saul. The Holy Spirit was in Saul now! It was a new beginning for Saul, so God gave him a new name—Paul.

USE THE FORCE

God, fill me with your Holy Spirit! I want a new beginning too.

DEVOTION 131

But Saul grew more and more powerful.
The Jews living in Damascus couldn't
believe what was happening. Saul
proved to them that Jesus is the Messiah.

ACTS 9:22

MASTER MOMENT

Paul made many new friends. Spreading
Jesus' message is a good way to meet new
people.

WAYS OF WISDOM

Paul taught many, many people about
Jesus. People who believed in Jesus were called
Christians. Paul baptized these new Christians.
He taught them everything he knew about
Jesus. People were so happy to learn that Jesus
loved them and that he'd been willing to give
up his life for their sins.

USE THE FORCE

Thank you Lord, for your Holy Spirit. The
world is new! I am happy to be a Christian.

DEVOTION 132

So Paul stayed with the believers. He moved about freely in Jerusalem. He spoke boldly in the Lord's name.

ACTS 9:28

MASTER MOMENT

Paul spread God's good news around the world. We can do that too!

WAYS OF WISDOM

Paul traveled all over the world. He walked for miles. He talked to many people. Paul helped the new Christians start new churches. Paul's new friends worshiped God. They loved Jesus and were happy to listen to Paul talk about Jesus.

USE THE FORCE

Wherever I go, Jesus, I will tell others about you. Love for you stretches around the world. I want to do my part too.

DEVOTION 133

The king told him to bring him some of the Israelites ... They had to be well educated. They had to have the ability to understand new things quickly and easily. The king wanted men who could serve in his palace. **DANIEL 1:3–4**

MASTER MOMENT

Daniel grew up in a strange country, far away from home. But God was with him. He is always with us.

WAYS OF WISDOM

Daniel loved God. The king of Babylon took Daniel to his country to live. Daniel was very smart, so he was chosen to be a helper to the king. Even in another country, God was still with Daniel!

USE THE FORCE

Thank you, God, that wherever I am, you are there! Even when I am far from home, I can feel at home because you are with me.

DEVOTION 134

> Other men in his kingdom claimed to get knowledge by using magic. But the answers of Daniel and his friends were ten times better than theirs.
>
> **DANIEL 1:20**

MASTER MOMENT

The king was impressed with Daniel. God blessed Daniel with special wisdom.

WAYS OF WISDOM

Daniel studied for three years. Then he served the king. Daniel did a great job! God gave Daniel wisdom. Daniel could answer the king's questions better than the king's own people.

USE THE FORCE

Dear Lord, help me as I am learning to read and to write. Learning is not magic. I know I have to try hard. Thank you, God, that I can use my knowledge to give you glory!

DEVOTION 135

About midnight Paul and Silas were praying. They were also singing hymns to God. The other prisoners were listening to them.

ACTS 16:25

MASTER MOMENT

God will help us whether we are doing big things or small things for him.

WAYS OF WISDOM

Paul and his friend Silas worked together. They taught people about Jesus. One time, some people who did not know about Jesus' love put Paul and Silas in jail. Other people might have been scared, but not Paul and Silas. They knew God would help them!

USE THE FORCE

God, thank you for your help for me, always.

DEVOTION 136

The jailer brought them into his house. He set a meal in front of them. He and everyone who lived with him were filled with joy. They had become believers in God.   **ACTS 16:34**

MASTER MOMENT

God takes care of those who love him. We can have faith that he will care for us.

WAYS OF WISDOM

When Paul and Silas were in jail, there was an earthquake. The doors flew open! The prisoners did not run away. The guard took them to his own house. The guard and his family heard about God and believed.

USE THE FORCE

God, thank you for the times when you rescue me. I will tell others!

DEVOTION 137

> Later, the woman had a baby boy. She named him Samson. As he grew up, the LORD blessed him. The Spirit of the LORD began to work in his life.
>
> **JUDGES 13:24–25**

MASTER MOMENT

Some people are strong on the outside, but true strength is on the inside.

WAYS OF WISDOM

Samson's mother raised her son to believe in God from the time he was born. That gave Samson strong faith plus the strength of God's love. Samson was blessed with great strength in his body. But the strength inside him was much more important!

USE THE FORCE

I praise you, God, for the strength inside me that comes from you! You give me real strength, dear God.

DEVOTION 138

> Then he prayed to the Lord. Samson said, "Lord and King, show me that you still have concern for me. Please, God, make me strong just one more time. Let me pay the Philistines back for what they did to my two eyes. Let me do it with only one blow." **JUDGES 16:28**

Master Moment

Sometimes even heroes can make a bad choice.

Ways of Wisdom

Samson was very strong. But then he made a bad choice. He did something God did not want him to do. He lost his great strength. But he did not lose God's love. He asked God to make him strong one last time, and God did it.

Use the Force

Dear Lord, I make bad choices, but I know I can always tell you, "I'm sorry," and you will forgive me. God, I praise you that you will give me more chances to make good choices!

DEVOTION 139

When Israel's army saw Goliath, all of them ran away from him. That's because they were so afraid.   **1 SAMUEL 17:24**

MASTER MOMENT

We don't have to be afraid just because everyone else is afraid.

WAYS OF WISDOM

The Israelite army was scared of Goliath. Not one man was brave enough to face the giant. Then David came into the camp. He was not afraid! Think about what might have happened if David had been afraid too! No one would have faced Goliath!

USE THE FORCE

Dear Lord, I am a child like David, but I know that anyone can be brave with you on their side. I praise you that I can be brave even if others are not!

DEVOTION 140

Saul replied, "You aren't able to go out there and fight that Philistine. You are too young. He's been a fighting man ever since he was a boy."

1 SAMUEL 17:33

MASTER MOMENT

You don't have to be a big person to have confidence in our great big God!

WAYS OF WISDOM

David was a young boy. But he trusted God. He knew God was always with him. David told King Saul that he was not afraid. David was ready to fight the giant Goliath. He wanted to show everyone how strong God is.

USE THE FORCE

God, thank you so much that you allowed David to know it was your strength inside of him. David knew this was not about his strength. I praise you, God, that I can be an example of big faith in a big God!

DEVOTION 141

The LORD saved me from the paw of the lion. He saved me from the paw of the bear. And he'll save me from the powerful hand of this Philistine too.

1 SAMUEL 17:37A

MASTER MOMENT

We have to trust God all the time, no matter how big the challenge.

WAYS OF WISDOM

David heard about the giant Goliath. His brothers were too afraid to fight. But not David! David believed God was bigger and stronger than any giant! God had always helped David before. David knew God would help this time too.

USE THE FORCE

David had faced lions and bears! I might never have to stare down a bear. But, challenges even come to kids like me. I praise you, God, for I don't have to do anything without your help!

DEVOTION 142

David said to Goliath, "You are coming to fight against me with a sword, a spear and a javelin. But I'm coming against you in the name of the Lord who rules over all." **1 SAMUEL 17:45**

master moment

God gives us the right weapons to fight for him. Our best weapon is prayer!

ways of wisdom

David chose stones and a slingshot to use when he fought Goliath. But more important than those things, David had faith in God. He prayed to God. Then he knew in his heart that God would take care of everything. And God did! David beat Goliath in the fight. Think about how strong you could be if you believed and prayed to God like David!

use the force

Even children have jobs to do. God, I praise you for prayer! Help me to always pick prayer for my first and best tool for any job.

DEVOTION 143

The LORD is my shepherd. He gives me everything I need.   **PSALM 23:1**

MASTER MOMENT

The Lord is our shepherd. He watches over our lives.

WAYS OF WISDOM

David wrote down his thoughts about God. David thought of God as a good shepherd who was always watching over him. Like a good shepherd guides his sheep, God guides us toward the right paths. He gives us what we need. God's love and goodness are with us every day, forever. David knew this, and he wrote it down.

USE THE FORCE

I praise you, God, for giving us the ability to write and draw about your goodness. Just like David, I can write, sing, and, most of all, pray to thank you for your goodness.

DEVOTION 144

Jesus reached the spot where Zacchaeus was. He looked up and said, "Zacchaeus, come down at once. I must stay at your house today."

LUKE 19:5

master moment

Jesus accepts all people. He accepted Zacchaeus. He accepts you too.

ways of wisdom

Jesus saw Zacchaeus up in the tree. Jesus wanted to talk with him. The other people were surprised. They didn't like Zacchaeus. But Jesus still wanted to go to Zacchaeus' house.

use the force

Jesus, you care about people, not about what is popular. What is popular comes and goes. Help me to remember that when others around me cannot.

DEVOTION 145

Do everything the LORD your God requires.
Live the way he wants you to. Obey his
orders and commands. Keep his laws
and rules. Do everything written in the
Law of Moses. Then you will have success
in everything you do. You will succeed
everywhere you go.   **1 KINGS 2:3**

MASTER MOMENT

Parents who love God will pass on their faith
to their children.

WAYS OF WISDOM

One of King David's sons was named
Solomon. David taught Solomon to love God
very much. David wanted Solomon to be the
king of Israel after him. When David died,
Solomon became the new king.

USE THE FORCE

I praise you, God, for my parents who help
me to learn about you! Teaching children about
you is a big job. Help me, God, to always respect
my mother and father.

DEVOTION 146

I will give it to you. I will give you a wise and understanding heart. So here is what will be true of you. There has never been anyone like you. And there never will be.

1 KINGS 3:12

MASTER MOMENT

When God gives us wisdom, other people will notice!

WAYS OF WISDOM

God made King Solomon very wise. Solomon made many wise decisions. He wrote wise sayings called proverbs to teach others what was right and true. People from all over the world came to hear Solomon's wisdom. God used King Solomon to show us how important wisdom is for us. We can ask for the gift of wisdom.

USE THE FORCE

God, I will be learning so much as I grow up! How will I make sense of it all? I will ask for wisdom. I praise you, God, for teaching me to be wise!

DEVOTION 147

Sometime later the brook dried up. It hadn't rained in the land for quite a while. A message came to Elijah from the LORD. He said, "Go right away to Zarephath in the region of Sidon. Stay there. I have directed a widow there to supply you with food." **1 KINGS 17:7–9**

MASTER MOMENT

Sometimes God will send one of his special servants into our lives to help us.

WAYS OF WISDOM

God has special servants everywhere, all the time. When we need someone like that, God makes sure to send us a helper! One of God's special helpers from long ago was the prophet Elijah. God sent Elijah to meet and help a poor widow who was very hungry.

USE THE FORCE

I can help others! I praise you, God, for making me, a child, able to serve others!

DEVOTION 148

The woman said to her husband, "That man often comes by here. I know that he is a holy man of God. Let's make a small room for him on the roof. We'll put a bed and a table in it. We'll also put a chair and a lamp in it. Then he can stay there when he comes to visit us." **2 KINGS 4:9–10**

MASTER MOMENT

The best friends are the ones with whom you can share your love of God.

WAYS OF WISDOM

Elisha worked hard for God. He made some good friends. One couple even set up a room just for him. They knew Elisha was a man of God. They wanted him to have a special place to stay. It is good to have friends who love God.

USE THE FORCE

Friends are gifts from you, God. Thank you for friends to share our faith in you with. Together we praise you, God!

DEVOTION 149

[Elisha] said to Gehazi, "Tell her, 'You have gone to a lot of trouble for us. Now what can we do for you? Can we speak to the king for you? Or can we speak to the commander of the army for you?'"

2 KINGS 4:13

MASTER MOMENT

It is good to be kind to God's helpers.

WAYS OF WISDOM

God gave his prophets some special skills and knowledge. The prophets could use those skills or knowledge to help people. Elisha wanted to make sure that the woman and her husband who helped him knew he was grateful. He wanted them to feel God's love too.

USE THE FORCE

I praise you, God, that I can help others feel your love! I will be a helper for you.

DEVOTION 150

If that is how God dresses the wild grass, how much better will he dress you! After all, the grass is here only today. Tomorrow it is thrown into the fire. Your faith is so small!   **LUKE 12:28**

MASTER MOMENT

God makes the beautiful flowers of the field bloom. So we don't have to worry. He will take care of our needs too!

WAYS OF WISDOM

God never ignores us or what we need. We were created in his image, so we are very special to him. God does not want us to worry about things like food and clothes. God knows just what we need. He gives that to us, and more!

USE THE FORCE

God, you take good care of me! I don't need to worry. That is a wonderful feeling to have.

DEVOTION 151

Finally these men said, "We want to bring charges against this man Daniel. But it's almost impossible for us to come up with a reason to do it. If we find a reason, it will have to be in connection with the law of his God."   **DANIEL 6:5**

MASTER MOMENT

Daniel was a faithful man who loved to pray to God.

WAYS OF WISDOM

Daniel was King Darius' best helper. But the other helpers did not like Daniel. They thought of a way to hurt Daniel. Daniel loved God. So the other helpers got the king to make a law that said people could pray only to the king.

USE THE FORCE

I praise you, God, for faithful followers! Help me to be a faithful follower, even if bullies try to change my mind. Please continue to bring people like Daniel into my life.

DEVOTION 152

[Daniel] did just as he had always done before. He went home to his upstairs room ... He got down on his knees and gave thanks to his God. **DANIEL 6:10**

MASTER MOMENT

Daniel prayed to God every single day at least three times a day. We should talk with God every day!

WAYS OF WISDOM

The king was talked into making a new law. No one could pray to anyone except him or they would be thrown into the lions' den. Daniel would never follow that rule! He loved God. He wanted to praise God every day. Daniel did not care about the new law. He went home and prayed to God.

USE THE FORCE

Lord, I want to be like Daniel. I promise to pray to you every day!

DEVOTION 153

They said, "Your Majesty, didn't you sign an official order? It said that for the next 30 days none of your people could pray only to you ..." The king answered, "The order must still be obeyed. It's what the laws of the Medes and Persians require. So it can't be changed." **DANIEL 6:12**

MASTER MOMENT

Daniel was arrested for obeying God's laws. Obeying God should be important no matter what the consequences.

WAYS OF WISDOM

Daniel did not stop praying to God. So some men arrested him. They brought Daniel to the king. The king loved Daniel, but he had to follow his rule. Daniel's love of God got Daniel into trouble. But Daniel was brave. He believed that God would help him.

USE THE FORCE

I praise you, God, that you are there when it gets hard to be your follower!

DEVOTION 154

So the king gave the order. Daniel was brought out and thrown into the lions' den. The king said to him, "You always serve your God faithfully. So may he save you!" **DANIEL 6:16**

MASTER MOMENT

Even when things go wrong, God has not forgotten us.

WAYS OF WISDOM

Daniel was thrown into the lions' den. This was not good news. But God knew what was happening to Daniel. God knew how strong Daniel's faith was. And Daniel knew how strong God was! Daniel trusted God. He knew what was happening was part of God's plan.

USE THE FORCE

Dear Lord, sometimes I am just as afraid as Daniel must have been in that lions' den. I tremble. I cry. Then I remember that I can count on your unfailing love, God! I praise you!

DEVOTION 155

When he got near it, he called out to Daniel. His voice was filled with great concern. He said, "Daniel! You serve the living God. You always serve him faithfully. So has he been able to save you from the lions?" **DANIEL 6:20**

master moment

God's miracles are for everyone to see. They are God's way of showing his love and care.

ways of wisdom

The king knew how strong Daniel's faith in God was. In the morning, he ran to see if his friend Daniel was safe. Daniel was alive! He wasn't even hurt. God had sent angels to hold the lions back. The king knew it was a miracle! The king praised the God of Daniel!

use the force

I praise you, God, for showing your love and care to the whole world!

DEVOTION 156

Jesus asked, "Weren't all ten healed? Where are the other nine?"

LUKE 17:17

MASTER MOMENT

Saying thank you is very important. We should not forget to thank God!

WAYS OF WISDOM

Jesus healed ten sick men. The men felt great. They were filled with joy. One man came back. He said, "Thank you so much!" Jesus wondered why only one man came to thank him.

USE THE FORCE

Do not let me forget to thank others, God. I can thank them out loud. I can write a note or draw a picture. Giving thanks is important. Thank you, Lord, for the help of friends.

DEVOTION 157

Here I am! I stand at the door and knock. If anyone hears my voice and opens the door, I will come in. I will eat with that person and they will eat with me.

REVELATION 3:20

MASTER MOMENT

God lives in heaven, but he will also live inside your heart if you ask.

WAYS OF WISDOM

We know that God is in heaven. But he is here with us too. He is with us all the time. Ask God to come live in your heart. He will do it! He will listen to your prayers and be there for you. Tell God you love him and are sorry for your sins. He wants to be close to you. He loves you.

USE THE FORCE

God, you gave me a way to be united with you. I just have to ask! Dear God, please come into my heart.

DEVOTION 158

Naaman was army commander of the king of Aram. He was very important to his master and was highly respected. That's because the LORD had helped him win the battle over Aram's enemies. He was a brave soldier. But he had a skin disease.   **2 KINGS 5:1**

MASTER MOMENT

Sometimes our problems seem too big. We need help to solve them.

WAYS OF WISDOM

No matter how big or scary, God can help us with our problems. That is what we believe! That is what Naaman needed to believe too. Naaman had a bad skin disease. He couldn't cure it. Just when his problem seemed too hard, God stepped in to help him!

USE THE FORCE

Like Naaman, sometimes I think I have a better idea. Help me to listen to you, God. I know you will always help me!

DEVOTION 159

"Come and follow me," Jesus said. "I will send you out to fish for people."

MATTHEW 4:19

master moment

Jesus needed helpers to spread his Father's message of love. Jesus lets us help him too!

ways of wisdom

Jesus knew teaching about God was a big job. There were so many people to tell! Jesus wanted helpers. He looked for helpers who were happy to do hard work. He found some fishermen and said, "Follow me."

use the force

I am not afraid to work hard for you, God! Teaching in the church or teaching in the neighborhood is a big job. I am a child, but I can still help Jesus. Lord, help me to feel confident so I can help others.

DEVOTION 160

This is how you should pray. "Our Father in heaven, may your name be honored."

MATTHEW 6:9

master moment

There are many ways that we can tell God we love him. One way is to pray.

ways of wisdom

Jesus taught the people many things. He taught them about prayer. Jesus prayed, and he wanted the people to pray too. One day, he taught them a prayer. We call it "The Lord's Prayer." People can pray this prayer every day.

use the force

Our Father in heaven, may your name be honored. May your kingdom come. May what you want to happen be done on earth as it is done in heaven. Give us today our daily bread. And forgive us our sins, just as we also have forgiven those who sin against us. Keep us from sinning when we are tempted. Save us from the evil one. (Matthew 6:9–13)

DEVOTION 161

> Jesus went through all the towns and villages ... He healed every illness and sickness. When he saw the crowds, he felt deep concern for them.
>
> **MATTHEW 9:35–36A**

MASTER MOMENT

Jesus healed lots of people, but he didn't have time to meet every single need. He wants helpers!

WAYS OF WISDOM

Everyone wanted to see Jesus. Big crowds came to him. Jesus helped many, many people. But he did not help everyone. He prayed and asked his Heavenly Father which needs he should meet.

USE THE FORCE

Jesus, thank you for the force of your healing. I will take the Holy Spirit with me when I help my family or friends who need to be cared for.

DEVOTION 162

> [The king] agreed to the terms of the covenant in front of the LORD. He promised to obey them with all his heart and with all his soul. So he agreed to the terms of the covenant written down in that book.
>
> **2 KINGS 23:3**

MASTER MOMENT

The Word of God is the greatest treasure! It is a treasure to be shared.

WAYS OF WISDOM

A treasure is something special that we care for. King Josiah's men found a scroll hidden in the temple wall. It was the Book of God's Law! It was the best treasure they could have found! It was the Word of God!

USE THE FORCE

Your Word is a treasure, God. When I am searching for something to make my life feel special, I will look in the Bible. There I find endless treasure!

DEVOTION 163

It was very early in the morning and still dark. Jesus got up and left the house. He went to a place where he could be alone. There he prayed.

MARK 1:35

MASTER MOMENT

Jesus took special time out to pray. We should do that too.

WAYS OF WISDOM

Prayer was important to Jesus. He loved talking with his heavenly Father. No matter how tired or busy he was, Jesus always spent time praying. Jesus wants us to pray too. He teaches us how to pray. And we have many great reasons to pray.

USE THE FORCE

Dear Lord, I am here. I am listening. I need you.

DEVOTION 164

One day Jesus said to his disciples, "Let's go over to the other side of the lake." So they got into a boat and left. As they sailed, Jesus fell asleep.

LUKE 8:22–23

MASTER MOMENT

Even though he was God, Jesus took time out to rest from his work. We should too.

WAYS OF WISDOM

Sometimes we forget that even though Jesus is God's Son, here on earth he was also human! He needed to rest and relax just like we do. Jesus worked very hard teaching people and his disciples. Jesus deserved to rest. He knew rest was good for him.

USE THE FORCE

Jesus, help me to rest secure, knowing you are here and taking care of me.

DEVOTION 165

While Jesus was saying this, a synagogue leader came. He got down on his knees in front of Jesus. He said, "My daughter has just died. But come and place your hand on her. Then she will live again."

MATTHEW 9:18

MASTER MOMENT

It is never too late for God! Nothing is impossible with God.

WAYS OF WISDOM

A leader named Jairus needed Jesus' help. His little girl was sick. Jairus knew that all Jesus had to do was touch her. Then his daughter would be fine. Jesus knew that Jairus was filled with faith. He went with Jairus.

USE THE FORCE

Jesus, thank you for your miracles. I know nothing is impossible for you.

DEVOTION 166

> After the crowd had been sent outside, Jesus went in. He took the girl by the hand, and she got up.
>
> **MATTHEW 9:25**

MASTER MOMENT

Jesus will never let us down. His faith holds ours up.

WAYS OF WISDOM

The crowd told Jairus his little girl was dead. Jairus doubted his faith. Jesus went to see the little girl. He held her hand. Even though she was dead, Jesus told her to get up. She did! Jairus and his wife were so happy. Even when their faith was not strong, God understood and he helped their daughter.

USE THE FORCE

Thank you, God, for making it so easy to trust you. I have faith that you can do all things.

DEVOTION 167

He answered, "'Love the Lord your God with all your heart and with all your soul. Love him with all your strength and with all your mind.'" And, "'Love your neighbor as you love yourself.'" **LUKE 10:27**

MASTER MOMENT

Jesus helps me to understand whom I should take care of. Everyone is my neighbor!

WAYS OF WISDOM

One day, a man said to Jesus, "I know I have to love God. I have to love my neighbor too. But who is my neighbor?" He meant, are only people like him or people who live near him his neighbor? Or are all people our neighbors? Jesus told a story about a man who was beaten up by robbers and left by the side of the road. Two men walked by the hurt man. Only one man stopped to help. Only one man loved his neighbor as himself.

USE THE FORCE

With your help, God, I will love my neighbor the best I can, even when it is hard.

DEVOTION 168

Then Deborah said to Barak, "Go! Today the LORD will hand Sisera over to you. Hasn't the LORD gone ahead of you?" So Barak went down Mount Tabor. His 10,000 men followed him.

JUDGES 4:14

MASTER MOMENT

God makes us brave when we need to be. Then we can help others.

WAYS OF WISDOM

Deborah was a leader of God's people. She was a smart and brave warrior. She helped the Israelites follow God's instructions. God wanted his army to fight a battle. They asked Deborah to come along. She helped them win the battle!

USE THE FORCE

God, sometimes you need me to be strong and brave. Sometimes I need to be like Deborah.

DEVOTION 169

What I'm about to tell you is true. Anyone who will not receive God's kingdom like a little child will never enter it.

MARK 10:15

MASTER MOMENT

Jesus wants adults to have faith like little children! He wants them to believe in things even if they cannot see them.

WAYS OF WISDOM

Jesus loves all people. But he especially loves children. He likes their faith in him. He told his disciples to let the children come to him. Then he said something surprising. He said that adults should become like little children.

USE THE FORCE

Jesus, you love little children like me! Help the adults around me to love you the way that I do.

DEVOTION 170

Say to the city of Zion, "See, your king comes to you. He is gentle and riding on a donkey. He is riding on a donkey's colt."

MATTHEW 21:5

MASTER MOMENT

From the time of his birth, Jesus was the one true King of Glory.

WAYS OF WISDOM

Jesus rode into the city. The people cheered. They cried out in praise to God. They shouted, "Hosanna! Here is our Savior!" Palm branches were waved in the air. People put branches and cloaks on the ground in front of Jesus and the donkey.

USE THE FORCE

Jesus, you are the King of Glory! Hosanna!

DEVOTION 171

By that time it was late in the day. His disciples came to him. "There is nothing here," they said. "It's already very late. Send the people away. Then they can go to the nearby countryside and villages to buy something to eat."

MARK 6:35–36

MASTER MOMENT

People are hungry for food. But people are hungrier to hear about God's love.

WAYS OF WISDOM

Over 5,000 people had come to see Jesus. He helped and healed many of them. The people were hungry and tired. Jesus' helpers were worried. But they didn't need to be. Jesus turned a small amount of food into a feast.

USE THE FORCE

Jesus, thank you for filling my hunger for God's love.

DEVOTION 172

> Here is a boy with five small loaves of barley bread. He also has two small fish. But how far will that go in such a large crowd? **JOHN 6:9**

MASTER MOMENT

God wants us to be willing to share.

WAYS OF WISDOM

Jesus said, "See if anyone has food to share." The disciples found a boy with two fish and five loaves of bread to share. They took the boy to Jesus. Jesus blessed the fish and bread. The disciples started to pass the food out to the people.

USE THE FORCE

Even if I have just a little, God, you make it so much more. And when I share, I feel your blessing! Thank you, Lord.

DEVOTION 173

So they gathered what was left over from the five barley loaves. They filled 12 baskets with the pieces left by those who had eaten. The people saw the sign that Jesus did. Then they began to say, "This must be the Prophet who is supposed to come into the world." **JOHN 6:13-14**

MASTER MOMENT

There is always enough with Jesus. He makes sure that each of us has what we need and more.

WAYS OF WISDOM

The disciples gave bread and fish to the people. It was amazing! There was more than enough for everyone. All the people were full, and there were twelve baskets of food left over. It was a miracle!

USE THE FORCE

Jesus, you give us everything we need, and so much more! Please help me to remember how much I have. Remind me to share the good things I have with others.

DEVOTION 174

When Jesus entered Jerusalem, the whole city was stirred up. The people asked, "Who is this?" The crowds answered, "This is Jesus. He is the prophet from Nazareth in Galilee."

MATTHEW 21:11

MASTER MOMENT

Some people do not like the idea of Jesus being the one true king.

WAYS OF WISDOM

Jesus was in the city of Jerusalem. Some leaders in Jerusalem were not happy. They did not like Jesus. They did not believe he was the King. They saw how the people loved Jesus. The leaders were jealous. They wanted to stop Jesus.

USE THE FORCE

Praise Jesus, the one true King! May others know that he is God's chosen one.

DEVOTION 175

> He went a little farther. Then he fell with his face to the ground. He prayed, "My Father, if it is possible, take this cup of suffering away from me. But let what you want be done, not what I want."
>
> **MATTHEW 26:39**

MASTER MOMENT

Jesus wanted his heavenly Father's will to be done more than his own will.

WAYS OF WISDOM

Jesus went to a garden. He talked to his heavenly Father. Jesus promised to do what God wanted, even though it would be very hard. Jesus prayed for strength. He loved all people. He wanted them to know God and to be able to go to heaven someday.

USE THE FORCE

Jesus, you promised to do what God wanted, even if it was scary. I pray I can be brave like you!

DEVOTION 176

"Put your sword back in its place," Jesus said to him. "All who use the sword will die by the sword. Do you think I can't ask my Father for help?"

MATTHEW 26:52-54

MASTER MOMENT

Jesus followed his heavenly Father's plans even though he could have stopped them.

WAYS OF WISDOM

The soldiers came to the garden and arrested Jesus. Jesus' helpers were very upset! They wanted to save Jesus. But Jesus stopped them. He knew he had to go with the soldiers. It was part of his heavenly Father's plan.

USE THE FORCE

Dear Lord, sometimes I do not understand. Why do some things happen the way they do? Even when I don't understand, I know your plan is right, God. Help me to remember.

DEVOTION 177

The soldiers brought them to the place called the Skull. There they nailed Jesus to the cross … Jesus said, "Father, forgive them. They don't know what they are doing."   **LUKE 23:33–34**

MASTER MOMENT

Jesus forgave those who mistreated him.

WAYS OF WISDOM

The leaders were not nice. The soldiers guarding Jesus were mean. They hit Jesus. They made him carry a heavy cross. They nailed Jesus to the cross, and Jesus died. Jesus could have stopped it at any time. But he didn't want to. It was all part of God's plan!

USE THE FORCE

Jesus, your life within me gives me life. Your life within me gives me the power to forgive. I can forgive those who mistreat me. Your love sets me free to forgive!

DEVOTION 178

The angel said to the women, "Don't be afraid. I know that you are looking for Jesus, who was crucified. He is not here! He has risen, just as he said he would! Come and see the place where he was lying."
MATTHEW 28:5-6

MASTER MOMENT

Jesus rose from the dead. He kept his promise!

WAYS OF WISDOM

Three days after Jesus died, the earth shook. An angel from heaven appeared! Some women went to visit the tomb. They were very sad. But they were in for a surprise! When they got there, they saw the angel. He said, "Jesus is gone. He is risen!" The tomb was empty!

USE THE FORCE

Alleluia! Jesus, you are alive!

DEVOTION 179

> Jesus came in and stood among them. He said, "May peace be with you!" Then he showed them his hands and his side. The disciples were very happy when they saw the Lord. **JOHN 20:19B-20**

Master Moment

What Jesus promised the disciples came true! His promises to us will come true too.

Ways of Wisdom

The disciples were hiding together. Suddenly, Jesus appeared! He said, "Peace be with you!" The disciples could not believe their eyes! Jesus was back! He was alive! How could it be? They touched his hands and feet to be sure.

Use the Force

Lord, your promises are true! Thank you for doing as you say.

DEVOTION 180

Again Jesus said, "May peace be with you! The Father has sent me. So now I am sending you." He then breathed on them. He said, "Receive the Holy Spirit."

JOHN 20:21-22

MASTER MOMENT

Jesus has big plans for us.

WAYS OF WISDOM

Jesus had risen from the dead! There was great joy. The disciples were so happy. Now they knew that God loved them. Jesus was happy too. He prayed and blessed the disciples. He had a big job for them to do.

USE THE FORCE

Jesus, you have given me your peace. I am ready to do my part. I will tell others about you and show them your love.

FIND YOUR
FAVORITE VERSE

Case for Faith for Kids

Lee Strobel

You meet skeptics every day. They ask questions like: Why does God allow bad things to happen? Can you have doubts and still be a Christian? Here's a book written in kid-friendly language that gives you all the answers. Packed full of well-researched, reliable, and eye-opening investigations of some of the biggest questions you have, *Case for Faith for Kids* is a must-read for kids ready to explore and enrich their faith.

ZONDER**kidz**